# NOELENE JENKINSON

# MAGGIE'S GARDEN

*Complete and Unabridged*

# AURORA
*Leicester*

First published in 2017

First Aurora Edition
published 2019

A catalogue record for this book is available
from the British Library.

ISBN 978–1–78782–077–7

Published by
F. A. Thorpe (Publishing)
Anstey, Leicestershire

Set by Words & Graphics Ltd.
Anstey, Leicestershire
Printed and bound in Great Britain by
T. J. International Ltd., Padstow, Cornwall

This book is printed on acid-free paper

# 1

Maggie Ellis drove into Tingara in the late afternoon. She had only been here a handful of times before but from now on this small historic rural town in the foothills of the Australian Alps would be home.

In the countryside driving in, pruned vineyards were at bud break producing new growth, tendrils and shoots before unfurling their fat lobed leaves. Bare trees were bursting into life again with their first covering of fresh green. On the town streets, avenues of ornamental trees frothy with white and pink blossom created a carpet of natural confetti beneath.

'Bees will be loving those,' Maggie murmured, feeling a conservative burst of hope for everything that spring's fertility signified.

She navigated the lively but narrow main thoroughfare, its streetscape lined with deep verandas over shop fronts, turned posts and lacy ironwork.

She sighed wearily, knowing that within minutes she could escape her loaded SUV after the three hour drive up country on the M31 from Melbourne.

Turning the vehicle down Stony Creek Way — her new address — to the broad cul-de-sac at the end, her heart warmed at the sight of her mud brick cottage, *Lakeside*, sitting small, proud and neglected toward the front of her acreage property with the Selling sign still up and a big red SOLD banner angled across it.

It had been on the market a while so Maggie had bargained a modest price, almost feeling bad for her tenacity because it was a deceased estate. Everyone else may have rejected it but the property was perfect for the vision she had in mind of starting a garden nursery business that she could operate from home. What the passer by didn't see from the road was the extensive land at the rear.

Although it was growing late, daylight would last long enough for her to unload, eat and sleep, and repeat the whole process again tomorrow with her second and last load. Within weeks, summer time would begin so she would have another hour of daylight to play with in the evenings.

Her nearest neighbour at a tolerable distance but on larger acreage lived in a big timber homestead and, according to estate agent Anne Perry, was apparently a truck driver. Outside was neat, she noticed, with mown grass but no garden. Anne Perry assured her the owner was a respectable man with kids, well regarded in the community and Maggie should feel comfortable having him around.

In the light of events this past year, Maggie had no intention of being anything more than distantly polite and would not be encouraging any new man, even a good neighbour, into her life.

She reversed into the driveway at the side of the cottage and parked. Groaning, she rubbed her aching lower back, stepped out and grew suddenly aware of friendly barking as a dog rushed toward her from the direction of the house next door.

Maggie loved animals but didn't have any pets in the city. With both she and Leon working full time, it hadn't seemed fair to imprison one in the apartment. Animals needed room to run and explore. Exactly what this Border Collie was doing.

The animal seemed friendly enough so Maggie approached it carefully and in a low gentle voice said, 'Hey beautiful. What's your name, huh?'

The dog wagged its tail, pricking up its ears at the sound of a sharp whistle followed by a man's growling command, '*Lady*!'

Maggie assumed he wasn't calling her. The sound carried on the crisp spring early evening air and the collie turned and obediently scampered away toward its master.

The man's outline emerged closer compliments of long easy strides. 'Didn't mean to bother you, Ma'am. She got away from me before I could tie her up for the night,' he explained as he clipped a lead on the dog, wagging its tail as her owner lovingly patted her at his side.

Big man, tall build with wavy sandy hair hinting at grey around the edges. Ruggedly handsome with a wide smile and clad in jeans, his checked shirt rolled up to the elbows.

'She's not a bother. She's gorgeous.' Maggie hesitated. 'I guess we're neighbours?'

His steady brown-eyed gaze wandered over

her from the top of her shiny shoulder-cropped auburn hair down to the Skechers on her feet. In her youth, Maggie hadn't generated undue attention from men and, these days, certainly not from married men like this one. And for the past ten years, having had a partner, she was considered out of bounds. So she found herself suddenly self-conscious. She had never been skinny even as a teen. Thanks to generous boobs and hips, she was what people considered *curvy*.

'Nick Logan.'

He extended a large hand as warm as hers was cold when she shook it. Clearly he either didn't feel the chilly air or was accustomed.

'Maggie Ellis.'

'Maggie,' he acknowledged with a quick nod. 'You okay here tonight? Have all you need?'

'Yes, thank you.'

He frowned. 'You alone?'

She figured she'd get used to that question eventually. Maggie's tired brave smile wobbled a bit but she hoped he didn't notice. 'Absolutely,' she said, trying to sound positive and happy about it.

He paused then said softly, 'We used to watch out for old Mrs. Black, too. We'll watch out for you. It's quiet here. You could feel isolated.'

Maggie vigorously shook her head. 'No way. I'll be too busy. That's why I bought this place because it was so peaceful.'

'Hope we don't disturb you then with myself, three kids, a dog and a truck all moving in and out of our place.'

No mention of his wife. 'You kidding? I love kids.'

His raised eyebrows registered surprise. That she liked children or that she didn't seem potentially bothered by the trucks? Her cottage had thick walls and double glazing, and she would be mostly working at the back of her property.

'Well I should get this girl home and leave you to settle in then.' He patted *Lady* again and ruffled her ears. 'Need a hand to unpack?'

'No thanks, I just have small stuff and I packed the boxes light.' With good reason, having to manage alone now. 'I'll be buying new furniture as soon as I can.'

'Welcome to Tingara. Need anything, just ask. Night.' He turned and walked away, leading the dog.

'Night,' she called after him.

Turning back to the cottage to focus on unloading, Maggie raised the rear door on the SUV and grabbed the first box. She had arranged for Anne Perry to organise the electricity to be connected so she crossed her fingers on one hand as she turned the key in the back door lock with the other and gingerly creaked it open. She patted the wall inside until she found the switch. Bingo.

Load by load, she carted in her few belongings, clothes and kitchen utensils as well as an inflatable camp mattress for a bed. The city apartment had belonged to Leon but, to her surprise, he had done one right thing at least and given her a settlement sum on separation even though they never married. His decision, not hers, she reflected bitterly.

Tucked away in an elite suburb, her florist

business had been a little gold mine over the years. She had sold it within weeks of the unexpected nightmare split and putting it on the market. Easy to get a buyer once they looked over her books and saw the steady healthy profits. Her SUV necessary for flower deliveries had been purchased within her first year and would now prove the ideal useful vehicle for her new business.

So, apart from what she had financially contributed to the household equally with Leon, she had saved her profits against a rainy day. Thinking motherhood but instead never suspecting it would be one like this. How foolish she had been.

But as much as Maggie loved being a florist she had always longed to establish a nursery of her own. Play in dirt, sow the seeds herself, nurture them into seedlings and plants for both the wholesale and retail market.

So, here she was. But enough maudlin reflection. She must stay positive. She wasn't over the hill. Yet. A new scarily exciting life lay ahead for her with a secret promise she cherished. Since her life was so abruptly turned upside down in the past year, she soon discovered it was never too late to start again in every way.

Finally, Maggie dragged the camping mattress and doona into the larger of the two front bedrooms, both with gorgeously ornate open fireplaces, and set up to sleep. After unpacking the microwave to cook a frozen meal and the electric jug to boil for a large mug of tea, she sat cross legged on the threadbare carpet — to be replaced — on the sitting room floor. The lovely room with French doors ran with the dining area and kitchen across the rear of the cottage. When she completed her garden transformation it would have stunning views in every direction.

Darkness fell and it grew quiet except for a dog barking somewhere nearby. *Lady* perhaps? Remaining positive, Maggie reminded herself that she wouldn't always be alone. Craving sleep after an early start, hours of packing up with her bestie and childhood school friend, Penny's help, the long drive and unpacking had left her pleasantly bushed.

She shivered at the thought of slipping out of her warm clothes in the chilly house so she didn't undress but stayed in her comfortable trackies instead.

Maggie had just snuggled under the covers and was anticipating the thought of a deep and hedonistic night's sleep when her mobile rang. Groaning, she struggled to sit up and check the caller. Penny. Equally single but in her case by choice. A librarian by day, inspired by gossip and living contently with her cats. In times past a woman who would have been safely labelled a spinster.

'Hey Pen,' Maggie said indifferently, feeling bad for a less then cordial greeting, seeing herself still attached to the phone in an hour when her body desperately longed for sleep. Penny's long conversations were notorious.

'I thought you might call me.'

Maggie sighed. 'Been a bit of a long day. I'm

in bed trying to sleep,' she hinted.

'You've arrived safely, then. You're not scared and lonely?'

Tingara was only three hours away but to Penny that meant outer space. Maggie had never known anyone less adventurous.

'Hell no. It's called freedom, Pen. I have my own life now at last. The house is empty but clean and my voice echoes around the room. I'll be back as planned tomorrow but the day after I need to do some serious cleaning and shopping for supplies here.'

Penny muttered something about *tree change* and *mad* but Maggie ignored her grumbles. Her friend was resentful because this move meant she was losing one of her few friends.

'The kitchen and bathroom need updating,' Maggie continued. 'There's an adorable old Aga set into the original brick fireplace. I'll clean it up and get it going in the morning. If I can find firewood. I'm too buggered tonight. It's more chilly here than the city. The air has a crispness to it that's invigorating. September is the perfect time to get my nursery established,' she prattled with enthusiasm.

'You'll die of boredom in the bush. You need to be busy.'

'Setting up a nursery will take care of that,' Maggie chuckled.

'You had such a social life with Leon.'

'His life not mine. I just went along with it waiting for the day when he gave me the nod so I could get pregnant, ditch that life and focus on being a mother.'

'Not a crime to be single, Maggie,' Penny disagreed. 'You'd do well to remember that and stop putting pressure on yourself to achieve something that might never happen.'

She knew her friend meant their single status and lack of children but Maggie chewed her lip feeling guilty for not being totally honest about her new situation.

'I get that, Pen,' she sighed, 'but deep down I know I was born to be a mother. I want children. I'm knocking on the door with the number forty on it. My ovaries will go into hibernation any day now.' Maggie imagined Penny yawning with boredom. 'We've been over this before. Don't worry for me. I'll be fine.'

'See you tomorrow then.'

'Thanks for all your help, letting me share your flat these past months and using your garage to store my stuff. I'll text tomorrow when I'm getting close to the city again, okay?'

'Don't forget to come back and visit,' Penny said.

'You can always come here to stay. I have a spare room. Tingara is not the outback.'

'If you say so. Night, Mags.'

The morning sun streamed through thin old curtains, easily replaced, Maggie thought, squinting against daylight after a cosy night's sleep. First things first. Light the Aga to dispel the dampness in the air and warm the cottage.

As she took a quick splash in the freezing bathroom, standing in the old pink bath beneath an ancient shower rose, Maggie mentally visualised her renovation. Gut the room. New tiles. New white basin and counter top beneath an antique framed mirror with a gleaming white freestanding bath and walk in shower.

Dressed in the same trackies again, she headed outside into the brisk morning, stepping over her sad garden and long grass making her way down to the creek, its low banks lined with gum trees. She gathered an armful of dropped twigs and branches, perfect to get a fire started. Maggie added a load of wood to her expanding mental shopping list of *immediate things to do*.

After a successful rummage down by the creek that gurgled along the back of her property, the kitchen fire soon blazed, instantly transforming the atmosphere indoors from cold and uninviting to warm and welcoming. She didn't feel like breakfast so, once the kettle boiled and fuelled by a big mug of hot tea, Maggie roamed her backyard that would one day be an awesome garden and thriving nursery overlooking the creek.

Her greenhouse would be erected at the bottom but further up closer to the cottage she imagined vines, creepers over arches and pergolas that would be lush green in spring and summer but turn a fiery ruby red in autumn. Sweet peas and roses would twine and scramble over lattice and there would be tubs of flowering plants, a dedicated herb garden, drift rows of lavender and coloured leaf seasonal plants. Massed floral borders crammed with plants around the garden edges.

Further down toward the creek a flowering golden wattle tree lit up its surrounds, a splash of gold against the olive green bush. She paused to admire it, sipping her tea as a kookaburra set up its raucous early morning laughing. Magpies joined in and carolled nearby.

Momentarily diverted by the lovely crisp bush sounds that echoed all around her, Maggie turned her attention back to her garden. She had space for a short allée that could lead to a fountain so the sound of running water was heard everywhere, the low trees perhaps under planted with seasonal bulbs so there was always something flowering throughout the year.

Maggie's hands quite literally itched to get to work. She turned to look back at the cottage where the whole colourful scene would have the backdrop of her historic mud brick home with garden views from every window.

The finishing touches would be a selection of well-placed cottage garden features. Rustic ornaments, benches and chairs, bird baths and a sundial. She aimed to make her nursery not only a place to sell plants but showcase what could be done. The small front garden she would transform into a riotous abundance of colour. The front door she decided she just might paint red!

Shelving her daydreams for the moment, Maggie finished her tea, locked the cottage, refuelled the SUV at the local garage then headed back to Melbourne for the final load of her belongings. After hours of packing and a quick farewell hug to Penny, she returned to Tingara after dark. This time to stay. She had stopped to stretch and grab a quick meal on the way to break the long drive, looping off the freeway at Seymour and eating lunch in a pretty park area in the main street.

When she finally arrived at the cottage, *home* she reminded herself, and entered its lovely welcoming warmth, although her surroundings were still strange, she felt brighter about this big life-changing decision and move.

Next day, it was well into the afternoon before Maggie finished unpacking and cleaning then drove down to the main street for supplies and browsing for furniture.

In a collectibles store, she found a round antique timber table and chairs hiding in a corner and a pair of comfy padded sofas in a back room, to be delivered the following day. She ordered a bed from a small furniture shop which meant a few more nights on the floor but it would be worth the wait.

Her small new refrigerator arrived at the cottage as she returned but Maggie's delight was tempered when she found the cul-de-sac filled with boys buzzing around on mini motor bikes and wobbling around the court on bicycles doing continuous laps. All seemingly heedless of traffic and none wearing helmets. With *Lady* leaping and barking around them, they must be Nick Logan's sons for no one else lived close.

Concerned for the children's safety, Maggie unlocked the cottage for the men to unload the fridge and marched back out onto the street.

'Shouldn't you all have helmets?' she shouted to the oldest boy on the mini bike, not even sure he heard above the noise. Growing aware of her presence in the street he slowed the bike to idle. 'Are you even licenced to ride on a public road?'

He glared at her in challenge. 'I always ride here.'

Maggie decided not to take it any further. 'Are your parents home?'

'Dad's out driving. He'll be home soon,' the smallest one piped up.

'What about your mother?'

'She doesn't live here. Mum and Dad are divorced.'

Maggie was surprised to hear it but it explained no previous sighting or mention of a woman about the property. Was Nick raising his sons alone? 'Who's minding you all then?'

'No one,' the tallest said. 'Zoe was supposed to but she didn't turn up again. I'm the oldest. I can watch out for my brothers,' he added defiantly.

The middle boy had stopped riding and just looked on in silence with the dog sitting on her haunches, panting, head tilted to one side, watching the proceedings.

'That's our dog, *Lady*. She's the only girl in the house,' the smallest one said, grinning.

'We've met.' Maggie bent down and patted her. 'I know this is a court and not much traffic but you're all old enough to be more careful out here on the road. I'll be driving in and out, coming and going in my vehicle now. When I open my garden nursery there will be more cars, too. I hope,' she added quietly to herself.

Their community street gathering was interrupted by the reverse beeping from the furniture van in Maggie's driveway and the approach from the direction of town of a familiar shiny white ute.

'Daddy's home,' the small boy cried out, beaming, *Lady* streaking along beside him as both ran towards it.

'Stop!' Maggie yelled with a hand on her chest in alarm.

The boy whirled around in surprise but Nick had pulled up at the roadside further back, clearly seeing the chaos. He peeled his long limbs from the ute and strode toward the gathering, taking his youngest son's hand as he approached.

'Evening, Maggie,' he drawled, nodding to her and easily addressing her like a long-time friend. 'These are my boys Tyler, Christopher and Noah.' He pointed out each one from oldest to youngest. 'What do you say, son?' he said to the oldest who had been zipping about on the mini bike.

The boy managed a mumbled apology of sorts loaded with resentment. With the roadway free now, Nick parked and the boys all off their bikes, the delivery van was able to leave.

The driver wound down his window and called out to Maggie. 'Left the invoice in the kitchen.'

'Thanks. I'll come by and pay tomorrow.' She waved him off.

With peace restored, Nick said casually, 'We're not used to having a neighbour. Old Mrs. Black didn't drive and *Lakeside's* been empty for a year since she died.'

'Fair enough but this is my home now,' she said firmly, refusing to be influenced by this man's quiet charm and knowledge that he was a single dad. 'I'll take every care coming and going but your boys need to be knowing their road rules and taking responsibility, too.'

'I agree.' Nick looked weary and his dipped frown showed annoyance. 'I'll talk to the boys. It shouldn't have happened. They know better.'

His scowl covered them all but Tyler in particular who Maggie guessed had probably misled his brothers and pushed the limits.

'Where's Zoe?' The oldest shook his head. 'Where's your helmet?' he growled. The lad glowered at his father and wheeled his mini bike back toward their house without a word. 'Why are you boys out on the street anyway?' He addressed the remaining two. 'You have plenty of room out the back paddock.'

'Zoe's not here so Tyler said it was okay,' the smallest, Noah, said innocently running around his Dad.

'Did he now?' Nick looked furious. 'You boys go on home and clean up for dinner. Chris, there's pizza in the ute.'

Maggie watched the boys saunter away, their voices floating on the evening air as they grumbled all the way back to the house. She shook her head and grinned. That Tyler looked like a handful. The middle boy, Chris, was quiet but observant, and the young one, Noah, was cute and honest.

Nick scratched his head and planted his hands on his hips, feet astride. 'Apologies for all this.'

15

He waved an arm vaguely about. 'Just had a thought for you though. There's a small shop in Main Street, nursery and florist, run by an elderly woman, Ivy Ashford. Not sure how much longer she can manage but you might want to go introduce yourself. She's a walking botanical marvel apparently. Loves gardening but not people, if you get my drift. Crusty old thing but her bark is worse than her bite.'

Maggie thanked him for the tip and promised to go meet her. 'Maybe we can help each other.'

Her mind jumped ahead to possibly supplying Ivy with plants as a potential shop front retail outlet market. She might even approach the local hardware store as well. Keep things local. If she supported them, hopefully they would return the favour and they would all benefit from mutual business.

'You best go eat those pizzas while they're still hot.'

'Obliged for your understanding, Maggie.'

Damn but she was getting used to him using her name. Seemed too personal since she hardly knew him yet but they were neighbours.

'See you around,' he murmured, heading back to the ute.

She surely would.

# 2

Using her freshly bought supplies, Maggie made a vegetable and pasta soup for dinner, writing the following day's job list while it bubbled on the stove.

Soon after shop opening hours next morning found Maggie sauntering Main Street in comfortable and flattering stretch fitted jeans, Skechers, a tee shirt and one of the long cardigans she favoured since she had long ago decided they slimmed her down.

She loved the independent owner-operated stores of small towns. No big chain or department conglomerates here. Not resisting the smells wafting out onto the street as she passed the bakery, she stopped for a mid-morning coffee and pastry.

Since a greenhouse and gardening supplies were her first business priority, she headed for the dimly lit old-fashioned hardware store that took up half a block on the corner of Main Street further down. Scrubbed timber floors, busy with customers. Always a good sign. As she browsed, Maggie noted prices. Reasonable. Hopefully she could strike a business discount for the bulk quantities she would need.

'Can I help you Ma'am?' a tall young man approached her in black jeans and a beige polo shirt with the store logo on the pocket.

'I surely hope you can. Maggie Ellis.' She

extended a hand. 'I'm starting a nursery from *Lakeside*, old Mrs. Black's cottage on Stony Creek Way. I was hoping to speak to the manager about supplying my business.'

He grinned. 'That would be my Dad, Ted Peters. I'm Luke. Follow me.'

He led her out the back to a large paper-strewn disorganised office with a computer barely visible somewhere beneath and a middle aged man wearing the same outfit as his son plus glasses. He looked over the top of them as they entered. Luke made introductions, explained Maggie's purpose and disappeared.

Ted rose from his chair and shook her hand. 'Heard *Lakeside* was finally sold. Welcome to town.'

'Thank you. Everyone's been friendly.'

'Have a good neighbour out there in Nick Logan.'

'I've met him and the boys.'

He frowned. 'Damn Rachel up and left him for some rich old guy. Don't make sense.' He suddenly shook himself from reflection and changed topic to go on, 'My ancestors started this store selling goods to gold miners in the early days of the town. Within a year there were 8000 diggers hereabouts and our family has been trading ever since.'

'Impressive.'

'Ain't meant to be. We love what we do and stand by our name.'

'That's rare these days.'

'Not in the country.' His grin threatened again. 'What do you need?'

18

Ted's office work may not have inspired trust but once he and Maggie began exploring, she soon learned he had his finger on the pulse of every item he sold. He just kept it all in his head instead of a computer. He offered wholesale terms plus a percentage, they shook on it and she started listing everything she wanted to start up.

'I need stakes, flexible piping to fit and miles of plastic poly covering for the greenhouse.'

'Done.'

'Delighted to see that soil yard out the back.' Maggie detailed the bulk mixes she needed plus pots, trays and work benches.

Ted wrote nothing down but Maggie suspected he'd get it right.

'We deliver. Want it today?'

She laughed. 'Tomorrow's fine.'

'Done. I'll set up a monthly account for you. Just need your mobile number.'

They finalised details in his office and Ted recommended a wholesaler in Bendigo where she could source everything else.

'They deliver too.'

'Brilliant. When I have plants ready, any possibility you'd consider stocking them?'

Ted didn't hesitate. 'Love to. Take all you've got. Let me know when you're set up and we'll talk price.' Again, he changed direction mid-conversation. 'Have to buy in a lot from Bendigo or the city these days. Dear old Ivy can't supply much anymore. You know, that old bird's eighty and ought to retire.' Ted chuckled. 'But what else would she do? She's fit and sprightly. Not really up to fully managing her shop any more though. No staff. Locals know she's slow and wait. Some tourists are more impatient and walk out but most accept she's a unique local icon.'

He sighed. 'I imagine being single it gives her life purpose after what happened in her youth. She loved old George Webster, business man in town, but it wasn't returned. Ivy was from a poor working class family. Her father was a market gardener. Where she got her love of gardening I guess. Anyway, she wasn't considered good enough. George married Annie from an equally well-to-do family and more acceptable. So Ivy lost her chance of love and never married.' Ted shook his head. 'Sad case.'

Maggie frowned and thought so, too. 'I'm about to go introduce myself.'

She shook her head as she left. As devastating as her own upheaval had been, she would never have let her broken romance define her life. But she also walked away in high spirits from the benefit of such local knowledge, friendly personal service and recommendations.

Ivy Ashford might be a different story, she decided, having been forewarned. So it was with caution that she stepped over the threshold of the only other nursery in town. The stone floor under her feet, every potted plant and buckets of fresh flowers in the shop was wet. Someone had just watered. *Inside?* An ancient manual cash register sat on the old wooden counter and a sign behind said *Cash Only*.

From the gloom toward the back a tiny woman appeared with a halo of frizzy hair and wearing a long baggy wool cardigan over a long dress with sensible black lace up shoes. Based on what Ted had told her and judging for herself now how quickly the elderly woman moved, she may look frail but was wiry and strong.

'Miss Ashford?'

'Ivy,' she squinted and snapped.

Maggie took a deep breath and, yet again, introduced herself and her plans.

'You from the city?'

'Yes.'

Ivy stared and grunted. Clearly in this woman's mind at least Maggie was cast as an outsider and the conversation promised to struggle.

'I've been in business here for over fifty years. I have goodwill from the locals. They all come here.'

*Okay. I've been told.* 'What about the nursery at Ted's hardware store?' Maggie probed.

Ivy dismissed her with a blunt, 'I have my regular customers.'

According to Ted, older residents probably that Maggie guessed remained loyal.

Ivy glowered in silence and the awkward conversation stalled. Maggie decided not to push it today. Exhausted, she didn't have the energy to spar. Hopefully she could get better acquainted another time. Ted would take her plants even if Ivy didn't.

Next day, wearing her favourite comfortable gardening gear of baggy cotton cargos, a long sleeved tee shirt and padded vest against the early spring chill, Maggie set about trying to fathom the logistics of her greenhouse construction. She sprayed the grass with aerosol paint, marking its position before she hammered stakes into place. Standing back surveying her work, and deep in thought, she didn't hear anyone approach until from the corner of her eye she grew aware of someone standing close.

She whirled around. 'Nick!'

She pressed a hand to her chest. Embarrassment overtook her surprise that she looked a mess but that went with the job and she wasn't trying to impress anyone here, right?

'Sorry,' he drawled.

Maggie pushed out a deep sigh of relief. 'It's so quiet and peaceful here after living in the city and working in a shop with the door open and constant traffic right outside, I'm discovering any noise tends to startle me. I'll get used to hearing only the sounds of nature and birds. It's quite lovely.'

Nick glanced about them at the pile of stakes and rolls of poly piping. 'See you're getting started already.'

'Ted delivered while I was still on my first mug of tea. Just marked out my greenhouse. Once I get it up, the floor down and shelving in, I can start planting out.'

'Lot of work.'

'Labour of love.' She grinned.

'If I'm around, any time you need help, just ask. I can send the boys over if you need them.'

'That's a generous offer. Thank you. I may take you up on it.'

He hesitated. 'I'm free now.'

'Really?'

He shrugged. 'Boys are all at school and I have an hour or two before a job later.'

Yet again, Maggie wondered how Nick juggled his driving and managing three schoolboy sons. 'Well, if you're sure, I need those stakes knocked in at the even distances apart I've already marked along the sides so I can start looping the pipes for a tunnel and covering it all with plastic.'

'Let's get started then.'

In his checked shirt, sleeves rolled up as always to the elbows, Maggie kept getting diverted by the sight of his thick muscled arms that easily handled pounding in the stakes. She sighed. So great to have a man around the cottage.

She took in his gentle sun browned face, the mark of a man who worked outdoors and was the target of those deep brown eyes gazing up to observe her warmly from time to time. He was genuine, strong and, no denying, remarkably good looking. Which she *had* already noticed.

When her handsome neighbour made it look so easy, Maggie questioned that she had ever considered doing the work herself. Focus, she reminded herself, and set to unrolling the poly pipe ready for the top framing. It would support the plastic covering to create the vast arched greenhouse tunnel space of her dreams and become the core work and growing area of her nursery business.

After only an hour when Nick had finished the stakes and brushed aside the sweat from his brow with his shirt sleeve, Maggie figured he would have to leave.

Instead, hands on hips and looking vital despite his labours, he glanced across at her and asked, 'What's next?'

'You can stay longer?'

He nodded. 'I reckon we can slot that poly pipe over together.'

'Sure but you must let me pay you later with a cuppa and fresh scones. Unless you're a beer bloke.'

Nick let his gaze settle on her face for a moment then said quietly, 'A coffee would be much appreciated.'

So they hauled piping into place, Nick cut it to size and within another hour they were done. While he washed up in the laundry, Maggie poured two big mugs of hot drink from the simmering kettle on the Aga and buttered the scones she had baked first thing this morning. Once she set to working, and as much as she loved food, Maggie tended to forget to eat and had long ago learned to get organised before she grew preoccupied and busy.

Nick ducked a little as he emerged from the laundry into the kitchen and glanced around. 'Cosy. Didn't get in here much when Mrs. Black was alive. She preferred her own company.'

'I know the feeling,' Maggie muttered.

They sat at the table where Nick soon demolished a scone in a single mouthful, washing it down with huge gulps of coffee to which he added milk and two heaped spoons of sugar. Maggie grinned to herself. Seems this man did everything in a big way.

'Surprised you're alone,' he commented.

Accustomed to such questions now, Maggie replied easily, 'I'm having a tree change. That's why *Lakeside* here on the edge of town suited me perfectly. Big block, plenty of parking space for my business once it's underway. But personally? I was dumped after a ten year relationship for a younger model. Walked away with pretty much only my pride.' How many more times would she need to repeat that?

Nick frowned. 'Man was a fool.'

Maggie chuckled. 'I think so, too.' She spread her arms, grinning. 'What's not to like?'

'Can't see a thing myself.'

A handsome man. Saying all the right things. Be too easy to lapse again. 'Thank you. What's *your* story?'

Maggie knew the gist from Ted at the hardware but was eager to hear more from the man himself and held her breath for his response, hoping she hadn't offended by asking.

Nick drained his coffee, his brow dipping into a frown as he glanced out through the French doors and across Maggie's work-in-progress garden. He seemed to struggle with a brief moment of self-consciousness before turning back to face her. Maggie had already discovered that the most personal of confessions never came easily. But after the first time, it gradually hurt less.

'Grapevine's probably already told you my wife moved on with another man. Older, richer and a distinguished kind of handsome.'

'That surprises me,' Maggie admitted. 'You're

what any woman would term a good catch.'

'You're good for the ego, Maggie Ellis.' He paused. 'You don't so much hate your ex as wish you'd never met them in the first place.'

'We all live and learn.'

He checked his wristwatch. 'Should be moving.' He rose and, clearly from the habit of a man accustomed to looking after himself, took their mugs to the sink, hovering in the kitchen and looking around. '*Lakeside's* going to need attention.'

Maggie smiled. 'Nothing major though, mostly cosmetic. A good look around didn't scare me. I kind of fell in love with it at first sight,' she admitted. 'Just needs painting which I can do at night and new flooring. I apologise for the laundry. I'll be replacing that hectic green paint with white, putting in a new loo and adding some panelled natural timber boards around the bottom half. It's great direct access from the garden. I'm sure I'll use it as a mudroom.'

'Lots to do. Don't forget we're neighbours. Happy to help out when you need muscle.'

'Thanks. Good to know. I'm available to return the favour and mind the boys any time. Watch out for them. I have plenty to keep me busy and grounded here in the next few months so I don't plan on going far.'

'About the other day,' Nick began awkwardly. 'The boys are good kids. Usually,' he drawled. 'Zoe used to be happier and more reliable but she seems down lately. Might be going through a rough patch or trouble at home. The girl comes from a big working class family,' he explained. 'I

26

know what that's like. She's the oldest of seven children and charged with responsibility for helping her mother to raise the youngest ones since childhood. Her father works two jobs, they don't own a car so he cycles to work and everywhere else in town. Rain, hail or shine, Zoe's mother walks everywhere.

'After Rachel left, I approached Zoe's folks about her staying with the boys after school. They agreed and at first she started out keen, was always reliable. But not lately.' He shook his head.

Maggie could see his obvious concern for Zoe. She gained the impression, Nick Logan wasn't a man who liked to fall short. Especially where his sons were concerned. By the sound of it he was trying to fulfil his role to be both father and mother.

'Life doesn't always go to plan,' Maggie mused, knowing how it could soon go awry when you least expected it. 'My offer stands. Permanently.'

Nick assessed her for a long moment, tussling with a decision. 'Obliged.'

'I love cooking, too, so I can sort out a meal any time.'

Since he tended to be serious, Maggie was surprised when Nick's face actually broke into a grin. 'We don't always eat pizza but sometimes it's an answer to a prayer. And we barbeque a lot.'

Loving seeing him more relaxed and less guarded, Maggie admitted. 'I love baking, and throwing everything into a dish together to simmer while I go outside and work. I make a lot of soup and casseroles.'

'Makes sense.' His grin was still there.

Silence fell between them. 'I should let you go.' Maggie rose, not wanting to delay her neighbour any longer. He had already been more than generous with his time. 'Thanks again. My greenhouse is half done already. I can cut and throw the plastic over the frame myself. Anchor it down.'

'Get stuck any time, you know where I live.'

As he turned to leave with an awkward half wave, Maggie thought of something else and called after him. 'I don't suppose you can recommend a reliable local builder for my renovation?'

'Mal Webster's the best around,' he said without hesitation. 'He's a busy man but it would be worth your while having a chat with him about your ideas. He lives in the blacksmith's cottage that backs onto Stony Creek the other side of town. His fiance, Emma Hamilton, is a jeweller in The Stables craft barn. Big old red brick building in Main Street.'

Maggie nodded. 'I've noticed it. Thanks.'

As Nick strode away, her feelings were mixed. He was a fascinating man of few words. Up there on the scale of good looks. Generous with his time but, then again, everyone had embraced her as a newcomer so far. Honest and trustworthy. Everything a woman could want. Except he already had what she craved for herself. A family.

But when she couldn't manage heavy stuff, she was wise enough to know straining herself was off the agenda and a risk she dared not take. Driven by her own urgency to get everything sorted by Christmas and year's end, it meant precious down time she couldn't afford. So, feeling comfortable with her neighbour, she would not hesitate to ask for his help.

More than satisfied with the morning's efforts on the greenhouse and keen to get her indoor renovations underway, Maggie drove around town to find the blacksmith's cottage and Mal Webster. With no answer to her knock and calling out, she headed to The Stables.

Meeting Emma Hamilton for the first time was a joy. The bubbly woman seemed to know all about her. Meanwhile, Maggie lost herself in jewellery heaven amongst Emma's beautiful creations, buying a necklace for her city friend, Penny.

Emma congratulated Maggie for being brave enough to start up a nursery. 'You mentioned you've already met our Ivy and it didn't go down well. She wouldn't have appreciated you coming into town. Her florist and nursery shop is her life. Living alone and single, she has nothing else. It gives her purpose. Keep trying. She's a grumpy old soul but she'll thaw. My gran, Mary, is a keen gardener. I'll give you her number.' Emma scrawled it down. 'I suggest you get them together and invite them over for a visit. They'll have a wealth of memories about your cottage and plant knowledge for you.'

'I'll add a cuppa and cake.'

'They'll be your friends for life. Ivy doesn't drive but Gran will bring her.'

Emma promised to tell her fiancé, Mal, to contact Maggie about the cottage renovations and suggested they catch up soon.

# 3

Next morning, Maggie had only just eaten breakfast, rinsed and dumped her tea mug in the sink and stepped outdoors to get started on the greenhouse covering, when she saw a white twin cab tradesman's ute pull up in her driveway, its tyres crunching on the gravel. A tall man with dark curly hair pulled himself up from inside and approached her with a wide cheeky grin.

'Maggie?' She nodded. 'Mal Webster.' She accepted his firm handshake. 'Emma sent me. Said you have a project.' His perceptive single glance took in the mudbrick cottage.

'I sure do but it's not as bad as it looks.'

'Reassuring. Never been inside. Apologies for the early arrival but thought I'd nip around for a quick look before I head out for the day.'

'Not a problem.'

'I can give you ten or fifteen now if it suits.'

'Come inside.' Maggie led the way via the front door, explaining her ideas for the bathroom and kitchen. 'I've had a surveyor in before the sale and he pronounced this dear old thing sound.' She patted a wall.

Mal thoroughly examined everywhere. 'Have to agree, and since it's just the two rooms, I can do it for you.'

'Great. Nick Logan recommended you.'

Mal grinned. 'Did he now? He's a top mate.'

'So, the cottage, I have a budget.' She named it. 'Doable?'

'Not a problem.' He hesitated. 'I'm working out of town on an historic property renovation for my boss all week, and Will Bennett and I are getting an eco-subdivision underway on the west side of town so I'll be consulting with him on a regular basis and project managing the site but.'

'Goodness, Mal,' Maggie interrupted with concern, 'are you sure you have the time for my job? I'm okay with it if you recommend someone else.'

Mal grinned and raised a hand. 'I can work on your cottage at weekends.'

Maggie frowned. 'But you'll have no free time. Emma won't mind?'

He shook his head. 'Weekends are her busy times at The Stables with her jewellery business and she's planning our wedding so it's all systems go at our place these days. I might need to bring my son, Daniel, with me when he comes to stay every fortnight though.'

'It would be a joy to watch out for him while you work. He can come play out in the garden. How old is he?'

'Six.'

'Wonderful.' Maggie's heart tumbled with delight. So many children in Tingara belonging to people she was getting to know. From having the prospect of no children in her life, there now seemed an influx of them in more ways than one. And, so far, all boys. 'It will be a pleasure. No rush on my job. Just do it as you can. I'm here all the time.'

'I'll call before I come.'

Mal lingered a few minutes longer, advising on appropriate heritage colour paint schemes for redecorating.

'I'll need to keep an eye on my budget of course but I intend to splurge on the latest style of bathroom and a marble surface for the kitchen counters.'

Mal chuckled. 'I'll order whatever you decide. You're the boss.'

Yes, she was now, Maggie realised, feeling a liberation she hadn't known for years.

A few days later and feeling more settled and positive, Maggie decided to confront Ivy Ashford again in her shop. She needed to get her business deals settled.

When she reappeared in the florist shop early in the day, relieved it was quiet with no customers, Ivy frowned. Nothing unusual there.

'Morning Ivy,' she smiled brightly. 'About my visit the other day? Won't take more than five minutes.'

No response just a mistrustful stare. Maggie pressed on. After what Ted had confided about Ivy's past lost love and sharing a vaguely similar history, she decided to dive right in and be equally blunt. Ivy didn't suffer fools and Maggie suspected she would respect that approach.

'I've been a florist for the past decade.'

'What went wrong?'

Maggie restrained a grin. 'With the business? Nothing. It flourished. Sadly my ten year partnership with Leon didn't. I was dumped for a newer model.'

Something flickered in Ivy's gaze which turned distant. 'Humph. Bloody fickle men.'

Briefly, Maggie imagined that her own life could have ended up like Ivy. But twelve months had almost passed and she soon learned that it didn't pay to let bitterness fester. She had made momentous decisions and moved on. Sadly, Ivy never had and Maggie's heart went out to her.

'Only some,' she said softly, sensing she had broken through Ivy's hard shell. 'I should thank him because it gave me the chance to start again and pursue my dreams.'

Moving on from the personal, Maggie reassured Ivy that her own small wholesale nursery business would be no threat to the elderly woman's livelihood.

'In fact, I'd hope to maybe complement your shop by supplying you with seedling and plants. Only if you want, of course,' she added tactfully, waiting for a response.

One or two customers browsed as they talked, probably locals because they greeted Ivy brightly but they only received a grunt in return. Ivy shuffled out the back of the shop and, for a moment, Maggie thought she had been deserted or forgotten, wondering if she had offended her in some way until she returned and thrust a sheet of paper at her, covered with beautiful and old fashioned cursive handwriting.

'My best sellers. Grow them. I want that paper back.'

Then she stalked away and busied herself in the shop, ignoring Maggie, their conversation apparently over. She grinned. Ivy wasn't so much intolerant as impatient. The sign of a deliberately busy, if unhappy, soul perhaps.

'I'll be in touch,' Maggie called out as she left.

That night, with Ivy's plant list beside her, Maggie delved into her gardening book and did some serious research on her laptop for wholesale seed supplies and where she could buy in base stock to take cuttings for the other species Ivy had recommended. She decided not to invite the local nursery doyen and Emma's gran, Mary, to visit just yet but wait for a few weeks until her greenhouse was fully built and operational when they could discuss terms of business.

It proved a struggle up and down a ladder but Maggie somehow managed to finish and anchor the greenhouse tunnel cover. Not because handling the plastic sheeting was heavy but because it was awkward dragging it into place over the poly pipe arches Nick had done with minimal input from herself.

Within days, she had set up her working height indoor metal benches and wooden pallet stands for pots, feeling the extra warmth and earthy smells inside the enclosure now. It was a vast space and Maggie grew excited at the prospect of filling it with thriving healthy plant stock. When established, it would all come alive with greenery and colour for sale.

She began by transferring countless wheelbarrow loads of potting medium and compost into large tubs, setting out her tools, pots, seedling trays and plant labels. It was all so handy to the house. She could nip into the cottage for a mug of tea any time.

For greenhouse watering, she decided on a simple shower hose system which would need a plumber to add a tap and connection. The process would be therapeutic, allowing her time to check on plants as she moved through. As opposed to more expensive and automatic overhead sprinklers.

Maggie became engrossed in transferring equipment and deciding workable placement for everything, Noah's sudden appearance surprised her. As he stood and stared at her uncertainly, she smiled.

'My word, you were quiet. I didn't hear you arrive. Are you sure you're not a pixie?'

He grinned and chuckled. 'No.'

'Where's your Dad?' she asked casually as she stacked pots.

'Out on a trip.'

'Your brothers at home?'

He nodded. 'They're playing footie in the backyard.'

'Zoe with you?'

He shook his head. 'She left early with her boyfriend, Jake.'

Maggie frowned. Nick had already expressed his doubts about the girl being inconsistent and that she hadn't always been so. Maggie wondered what influence had caused the change. The boyfriend maybe?

'How old is she?'

Noah shrugged. 'Don't know. Older than Tyler and she goes to the same big school.'

Maggie presumed that meant secondary and debated the wisdom of telling Nick that she was prepared and available to step in and watch out for the boys if Zoe failed him again. Which sounded likely.

'When will your Dad be home?'

'Soon I guess.'

Maggie realised, too, that the older boys hadn't missed Noah. He could have wandered off anywhere and no one would know where he was. 'You must miss your Dad.'

Again, Noah nodded, wide eyed and wary, clearly seeking out other company. Out of loneliness or reassurance, she was sure. She took comfort from the fact that he felt trusting enough to come to her. For the child's sake, she was more than happy to foster his friendship.

'And your Mum, too?'

Noah shook his head. 'We don't see her much.'

Was he seeking out another woman's company as a substitute? 'Well, I'm delighted you're here. I always appreciate another pair of hands and a man about the house,' she said, trying to make the lad feel wanted and valued.

Maggie didn't acknowledge that maybe having a boy like Noah around was feeding her need for the same thing. He shadowed her around the greenhouse like a lost puppy while she stacked pots, wondering what was quick and easy to make for a one-person dinner. Noah constantly asked what she was doing as she worked so she explained and gave him small tasks to carry things, encouraging him as they chatted.

When the lowering sun threw long shadows across the garden and the air chilled, Maggie suggested, 'Should you go home now? Be there when your Dad gets back?'

Noah shook his head. 'I'll hear his truck.'

Even as the boy spoke, they heard the distant rumbling of a diesel engine grinding down in gears, coming closer. Noah silently beamed at Maggie but made no move to leave.

Concerned Nick would worry if his youngest son was discovered missing, Maggie said, 'Should you be home so he knows you're okay?'

'Nope. I told Tyler I was coming over. He told me not to be a nuisance but I came anyway.'

Maggie clicked her tongue. 'Big brothers, eh?' They shared a knowing grin.

As she suspected, Nick soon appeared, frowning as he strode down the driveway and across the garden to the greenhouse, a shadow of stubble on his face. Clearly he'd had a long day and was looking frustrated, perhaps because his sitter had disappeared yet again, leaving his sons unsupervised.

'I talked to Zoe after the last time,' he explained. 'Apparently didn't listen.'

Maggie was tempted to ask why he persisted with the girl.

'Hope this boy isn't troubling you,' he said, rustling Noah's hair and pulling him close.

'Heaven's no. You're my little apprentice helping me, aren't you Noah?' The child glowed with pride. 'Not sure if he's too young to earn pocket money,' Maggie continued, realising how much she needed to accomplish in the coming months of spring, 'but if he's looking to earn a few dollars here and there, I could maybe do with help one night a week after school or a few hours on a weekend? But that would be up for discussion, of course.'

Noah craned his neck hopefully at the tall man he clearly adored. 'Could I Dad? Maggie's sowing seeds that grow into plants. She's a holtilavalist.'

Nick and Maggie exchanged glances, withholding grins, but didn't correct him.

'That a fact? We'll talk about it, okay.' He surveyed Maggie's skilled construction and swept a gaze of admiration around the enclosure. 'You've been working hard. Looking professional,' he said quietly.

'Thanks. It's taking shape.'

'With Zoe's new boyfriend Jake on the scene now, I'm hesitant to ask her for any night time sitting. She's probably out with him anyway. Besides, her mother will surely need her help with all the family home.'

Maggie nodded in understanding.

Nick brushed a hand over his face and combed fingers through his hair. Maggie didn't know Nick all that well yet but she would have sworn it was a self-conscious gesture and she grew intrigued to discover what was coming.

'Wondered if you're free tomorrow night to watch the boys. I . . . er,' he cleared his throat, 'have a date,' he mumbled, shuffling with embarrassment for either having to ask or that a divorced man with kids was putting himself out there again.

When it sank in what he was saying, Maggie's heart kicked over with a twinge of envy for the lucky woman. 'Oh sure. You work hard. You deserve time off.' She hesitated. 'Someone you're seeing?' She held her breath. Like it was any of her business.

'Probably just a once off. Guys talked me into it,' he drawled.

'So, I don't know Tingara all that well yet. Where does one go out on the town here?' Maggie tried not to feel extremely jealous.

'The Tavern. Kinda new and trendy rustic pub down the bottom end of Main Street. And a private party later.'

'Sounds nice. What time do you need me?'

'By six?'

'See you then.'

Nick took Noah's hand, gave a slight wave and Maggie stood watching the tall man and tiny boy disappear down her driveway back to the ute to the echoing sound of the boy's constant chatter. They looked so cute together.

About the same time the following night, Maggie wandered across the cul-de-sac in the dusk, the setting sun spreading filtered light through the gum trees and onto the roadway. As she sauntered up to the house, *Lady* greeted her first, barking in greeting and taking the broad steps up to the veranda alongside her. There wasn't a doorbell so she knocked.

Tyler opened it. 'Hey, Maggie. Dad's not ready yet. Come in.'

She tried to imagine big quiet Nick Logan fussing over what he wore on a date.

Maggie's quick glance flicked around the spacious country kitchen, usually the heart of a family home, she knew, judging by her own upbringing. Looked like the boys had already eaten. The crumbs and crusts of toasted sandwiches on the table and a sink full of dirty dishes told their own story. She had grabbed an early bowl of soup herself before wandering over.

'Your father go out often?' she couldn't resist asking, knowing she was digging.

'Nah. His trucking mates talked him into it. This woman has been hanging around, pestering him. He's her plus one for a big transport company thing.'

Then Nick appeared and took her breath away. Hair still damp from a shower, looking fresh, smelling of something deeply masculine. Her nostrils flared as he approached her across the kitchen dressed in black jeans, white shirt and a soft leather jacket.

'Looking a bit hot, Dad.'

It was the first time Maggie could recall Tyler looking like he had a sense of humour buried deep under all that anger and resentment, then he spoilt the positive mood by muttering unkindly, 'Wish you weren't going out with that woman though.'

'She has a name,' Nick said firmly. 'Mandy. Remember?'

'She runs everywhere, stinks of perfume and giggles a lot.'

'She's a busy girl and works hard in the community.'

'She's ditzy.'

His father was blunt. 'Tyler Nicholas Logan, I did not raise you to be rude or unkind. There's good in everyone, understand?'

Tyler scowled. 'Even Mum?'

The whole room fell silent as the other boys' glances turned in their direction from playing a game on the television screen. Maggie waited to see how Nick would respond.

Without hesitation, he said, 'She gave me three handsome sons and as the oldest, I expect you to set an example to your brothers, okay?'

It took a while coming as they glared at each other but he eventually mumbled, 'Yes, sir.'

Since the mood in the kitchen had darkened, by way of distraction, Maggie said lightly, 'Well, from where I'm standing, looking like that, no woman in her right mind would let you get away.'

'Then maybe she'll get drunk and forget about you.' Tyler gave a bitter laugh, trying to make a joke but his attempt fell flat.

From the puzzled look on his face, Noah had no idea what was going on, Christopher just slowly shook his head, knowing his brother well and staying silent, but Nick seemed to be struggling with control. Wisely for now, he said nothing. Maggie felt sure he must be disappointed in Tyler's attitude. Everyone knew the oldest boy had been out of line so there was no need for discipline. He had embarrassed himself by being deliberately unkind.

His father said with leashed patience, 'Mandy is not that kind of woman and you'll speak about her, your mother, Maggie and every female you encounter, girl or woman, with respect. Understood?'

42

'Sure,' Tyler snapped.

Nick was a strong principled male and Maggie doubted even Tyler's rebellion would ever win out against him. Because you respected the man, you listened to what he had to say.

For good measure perhaps, his father added wryly, 'Trust me, son, as you get older you'll discover there are a lot more fun things to do than getting drunk.' A twitch appeared at the corners of his mouth, as though he was reminiscing. Or anticipating his night out ahead.

Maggie privately sighed, wishing a man of such character would do more than glance in her direction. She fantasised that he would allow his gaze to linger, walk directly toward her across a crowded room, intentionally seeking her out. Really, genuinely care about her as Leon hadn't.

Her wayward thoughts were hauled back to the present when Nick rattled his truck keys, covering all three boys with a single sweeping glance and warned, 'I expect you all to behave tonight for Maggie and do your chores.' All three groaned. 'And since someone,' he glared at Tyler, 'has erased the last list from the chalkboard,' they all sniggered, 'I've written them out in pen on a piece of paper and stuck it on a magnet on the refrigerator. Ms Ellis will make sure it stays there,' he raised eyebrows and she nodded, 'and I expect every item to be ticked off complete when I get home.'

'Call me Maggie or you'll make me feel old,' she said.

In his childish innocence, Noah shook his head, smiling, 'No you're not.'

'She certainly doesn't look it, does she boys?' Nick said warmly making Maggie feel a ridiculous sense of worth and pleasure.

, He hugged each son, nodded to Maggie and headed for the door.

'Don't stay out too late,' Tyler teased as a parting shot to his father's back.

Maggie's perception of the all-male Logan homestead was of huge generous rooms, clearly built for a family, clean enough but untidy around the edges, perhaps only lacking a woman's touch. Although they appeared to manage well enough without one.

While she reminded the boys about their lists amid protests and moans, she set to washing the sink full of dishes, wiping down the kitchen table. Setting the room to right. In the living area further along, she picked up cushions from the floor, patted them plump again and replaced them on sofas.

When she was done, hands on hips Maggie watched Chris and Noah playing their game again on the television. 'So, what's the game?'

'Minecraft.' Chris' eyes didn't leave the screen as he replied.

'What's it about?'

'Chris is teaching me to make stuff and blow stuff up,' Noah's brown eyes so like his father shone with delight.

'It's about survival and achievements,' Chris put in quietly, for a moment actually taking his eyes from the screen. 'You discover things. Defend yourself. There's places to explore like ruins and abandoned mine shafts,' he explained.

44

'You go down caves to find stuff and finish the game.'

'Sounds addictive.' Maggie was way out of her depth. 'I'll stick to gardening.'

Noah chuckled but kept playing.

'Ten more minutes okay?'

Mesmerised by their game, neither boy responded. She shook her head. When time was up and she insisted on turning off the television, her order raised howls of protest but she ignored them, straightened a pile of motoring magazines, uttering firm reminders to the boys if they headed for the remote or a gaming device instead.

Over the evening, Maggie's initial perception of each boy was confirmed. She hardly realised Christopher was around and Maggie guessed he would become a strong quiet type like his father. Tyler was a hothead with issues but cooperative enough. Understandable in the wake of family upheaval but Nick seemed to have him figured and with respectful firmness pulled his oldest son back into line.

And little Noah? Flipped her heart. Innocent and obliging, tonight — as he had done yesterday appearing in the greenhouse — he trailed her about until she gently prompted him about his list. For the five year old it became a game and he mischievously chuckled his way through them all. Impossible to be mad.

When they were all done and in their rooms donning pyjamas and brushing teeth, Maggie found the laundry. By the time she returned from sorting and starting the first load to check on the boys, Tyler and Christopher bid her a casual goodnight, happy to put themselves to bed. Noah followed Maggie into his brothers' room clutching a ragged and clearly beloved book, then out again and into his own. Next to his father's room, she noticed, peeking through the half open door to see his unmade bed and a pile of clothes tossed over a chair.

Maggie removed her shoes and stretched out, sitting up against the bedhead quietly reading to Noah. He kept asking for more but finally grew drowsy and settled down. She kissed him gently on the forehead and switched out the light making sure to leave the one on in the hallway in case he was wary of the dark.

'Night, champ.'

With his eyes already closed, Noah muttered something and smiled as she left.

Maggie browsed the jumbled groaning bookshelves in the lounge, not surprised to see the Logan men were mostly a household of readers. Christopher was already a bookworm. Nick's encouragement, she wondered, doubting he would have much time to read himself.

When she heard his ute return and heavy footsteps on the veranda not long before midnight, he found her in a recliner with her feet up enjoying a cuppa and a book on landscaping. As she leafed through it, Maggie knew Nick had no time to put any of it into practice. Not for want of inclination, judging by all the masculine reading lined up on the shelves.

She hadn't given her automatic tendency to order and housework any thought until Nick's blank expression and sharp gaze clearly noticed some changes. His glance also drifted toward the closed laundry door and the sound of the washing machine's humming final rinse cycle.

'I appreciate you minding the boys but I didn't expect you to do our housework,' he said in a defensive tone.

Maggie winced. She had overstepped the mark on his territory. 'Sorry. To be honest, I prefer to be busy.' She brushed his comment aside as gently as possible. 'It's a cool night but I hung out one load under the back veranda and the next one's nearly done.' To distract any further objections to the way she spent her time while in his house, she asked brightly, 'I hope you had a good night?'

Nick tossed his keys on the counter. 'Yeah. Some.'

From his total lack of enthusiasm, Maggie figured his evening had not been a raging success or gone as well as expected but pride stopped him from admitting it. She felt for him. Everyone was unlucky in love at some point in their lives and often more than once.

To her surprise, Nick slowly shook his head and muttered, 'It was a disaster. She just wanted sex.' Catching her gaze of amused alarm, he said quickly, 'I didn't. Besides, I don't do one night stands. After a long working week and raising three lively boys, I don't have the energy.' Nick ran a hand over his weary face and pushed back his hair. 'She's another princess who wants a man to do everything for her. Hell, I'll respect any woman and especially one that takes my fancy but I don't have the time to be a servant.'

'Sorry.' She shrugged, waited a moment and said, 'I'm happy to come over and mind the boys whenever. Cook a one dish meal for you all if you're running late or short of time.'

He straightened and bristled. 'We can cook.'

'I didn't say you couldn't,' she said calmly, holding his gaze and gathering up her purse and house keys, realising she had offended him, wishing she could take back what she said, 'but you've been so generous with your time, helping with the greenhouse, being friendly, welcoming me to the neighbourhood. My offer was simply a way to say thank you in a way I know how. With food. It wasn't a slur on your ability in the kitchen.' Niggled and disappointed for no accountable reason, Maggie turned and walked away.

'Good night,' she called over her shoulder, feeling tired and disheartened, knowing she should expect this in her situation and working longer physical hours.

# 4

The cool night air hit Maggie's flushed embarrassed cheeks as she stepped out onto the veranda but before she had even reached the steps down to the driveway, the back door whined open and slammed shut. Nick's long strides caught up with her.

He touched her arm, forcing her to be civil enough to half turn and face him. In the dim light from indoors, she saw the genuine and sheepish regret on his face.

'Maggie, listen. I should explain.'

She crossed her arms, irritated beyond reason, confused to be feeling this distressed over a simple misunderstanding but willing to listen.

He sank his hands deep into his pockets. 'When Rachel left me for an old rich man, I felt like I'd been kicked in the guts. Like I wasn't man enough for her or a good enough provider. I work hard and earn a damn decent living. My boys want for nothing and I like to think that includes my love. I've also learned my way around a kitchen and I encourage my boys to do the same. Be respectful to women but not be stereotyped by gender.'

Staring at each other in the semi darkness, Maggie mellowed by his explanation, impressed. 'Fair enough. I appreciate you confiding in me and sorry if I was a mite touchy.'

'Truth is, Maggie, your efficiency and

capability makes me feel like a failure.'

'Oh Nick, you're not!' She impulsively reached out and laid a hand on his arm.

'Maybe but it's made me realise I can't do everything all the time. And I can't expect Zoe while she's still young to take on some of it. She's not fully mature and responsible yet. Plus she's been distracted lately by Jake.' Nick frowned. 'I don't believe he's a good influence in her life but I'd still like to give the girl a chance. Give her some pocket money for daytime and after school sitting.'

He shuffled his boots on the veranda. 'What I'm saying is I'd appreciate being able to rely on you sometimes as my backup. I know it's a lot to ask. You've only just moved here and I'm imposing on you.'

Maggie shook her head. 'Not at all. Just ask.'

'I'd pay you.'

Maggie scoffed. 'No need. If you can help me with jobs that are too heavy or beyond my handy-woman skills, that's enough of a trade for me.' She was thinking of her own needs, too, but raised a hand when Nick opened his mouth to protest. 'Just neighbours helping each other, okay?'

'How about a deal?'

She raised her eyebrows. This could be interesting.

'The boys and I sometimes do a cook up. Come on over one night for dinner and we'll *all* cook.'

The offer appealed but Maggie hesitated to respond. That would mean getting even more involved and closer to his family. Even offering

50

to mind the boys was pushing it but this man needed help and so did she. It was a mutual pay off. She could play it safe, keep her distance and stay neighbourly. After all, she had her own problems just as much as Nick had his. Life could get complicated. But with his honesty and admissions you couldn't help admiring the man just that little bit more. Maggie sighed. Just when she thought she had her own life sorted.

Seeing her indecision, Nick prompted, 'It's a big kitchen. Plenty of room for everyone.'

'I know,' she moaned. 'And you have that beautiful new bright red planetary mixer. What man goes out and buys one of those?' she added without thinking.

'Bought it for Rachel,' he admitted. 'Pretty much never been used.' He pulled a wry grin. 'Are we on for a cook up then?'

Maggie sighed in resignation. 'What's the deal?'

'Each person gets to make a dish of their choice.'

'Even Noah?'

'He's learning.'

'Sounds fair. What should I bring?'

'Whatever you want and keep it secret.'

'We could end up with five desserts!'

'My boys would love that. Food should be fun sometimes instead of healthy.'

'Day and time?'

'Weekends work best for us. Saturday okay?' The following weekend. Maggie nodded. 'About five-ish. Come when you need to.'

'Perfect.' Her voice and mood softened.

When he whipped her a cheeky wink, Maggie knew he would have been like Noah as a boy.

'Looking forward to it.'

Strangely, so was she, Maggie realised. 'See you then.'

As she strode down the driveway and across the cul-de-sac to her cottage feeling like Nick could be watching her every step of the way and not sure how she felt about it, Maggie acknowledged that the guy was too damned disarming. He was no womaniser but he was sure a role model for men and melting this girl's heart for seriously considering the opposite sex into her life again.

Maybe that was a positive thing. Might mean she was open to finding that elusive man of her dreams she fantasised about again somewhere down the track. Maggie smiled to herself in the dark as she let herself into the cottage. And it wouldn't be just her he was taking on. She would come with baggage.

Eager to get her nursery stock established, Maggie spent the rest of the week plunging her hands into organic loam, sowing hundreds of seeds and writing plant labels. Bathing in the extra warmth of her shelter on sunnier days or listening to the light drumming of rain on plastic as she worked, the number of filled trays quickly grew and seedlings sprouted.

She had always loved the smell of damp earth, being outdoors surrounded by nature and fascinated by the mystery and miracle of every growing thing. A legacy of idyllic childhood days visiting her grandparents on their small farm just outside the city.

When the sun emerged again from behind

bruised clouds, she took a break to gradually weed and tidy sections of her garden while the earth was moist. She was aware of Nick's truck or vehicles leaving and returning, getting to know the sounds of the engines. Sound carried in this quiet place. And occasionally heard *Lady's* distant barking or raised voices of the boys calling out at play.

By the weekend, her anticipation for the cook up with the Logans was high. She spent the morning in the greenhouse and the afternoon doing a food shop where she encountered a few familiar faces plus friendly smiles and waves in greeting. She had taken a huge gamble on Tingara but already Maggie felt like it would reward her for the decision. In time she hoped to be able to give back to the community that had so openly embraced her.

Toward evening as she prepared the ingredients for her chosen dish, Noah knocked on her back door but came right in.

'Hey champ.'

'I need parsley. We don't have any.'

'Sure do. You remember where it is?' Noah nodded. 'So you're making a savoury dish then?' Maggie probed.

His face broke into a gorgeous cheeky grin and he looked back at her on his way out to the fledgling herb garden. 'It's a secret.'

'Good thing I'm making dessert then, huh?'

'Dad bought a tub of ice cream especially. Just in case.'

'Maybe my dessert doesn't need ice cream.'

'Dad said every dessert needs ice cream.'

'That so?' Maggie grinned.

Although she was growing attached to them all, she was losing her heart to this lovable little son of Nick's in particular. As quickly as he arrived, Noah scampered away again clutching his handful of parsley.

Although she was enjoying the contact with other people's children by default, it was still no substitute for a baby of her own. Maggie crossed her fingers and sent up a silent prayer.

Because the cook up was casual but Maggie didn't want to appear too frumpy or homely, an impression she had always believed her generous figure tended to convey, she chose stretch fitted jeans. Any other time she would have added heels for a dressy touch and for some desperately needed height since the top of her head barely levelled Nick's face. Tonight, Maggie chose a silky plum coloured over shirt that followed and slimmed her curves.

So with sensible flat shoes and a prebaked fluffy sponge cake on an oven tray ready to be prepared and all the makings in a carry bag, Maggie wandered next door.

It seemed like lights shone from every window. Lots of noise and chatter drifted out from the kitchen into the crisp evening air as she approached the house. She knocked but wasn't heard. Her second knock was no more successful than the first so she let herself in.

Noah's face lit up. 'Maggie's here.'

Her heart warmed at the sight of his sparkling eyes and wide smile. One pair of eyes trained on her became four.

'Sorry, I knocked twice but there's so much action in here no one heard.'

Nick strode forward accepting her bottle of sparkling ruby wine. Maggie gaped, hooked on his appeal in a black polo shirt with the collar up and beige cargos. He was such a man, a typical outdoorsy kind of bloke. But on the other side of that, he oozed a quiet calm and sensuality. He could be touchy but that was just his male pride. A woman with lots of loving could ease that for him. Maggie blushed at her own thoughts. What was she thinking?

'Boys, make room for Maggie's stuff.'

They cleared a space on the kitchen island bench. 'It's dessert. I'll put it together at the last minute.'

'Now that's a tease,' Nick said softly.

As Noah chopped his way through cucumber, carrots, peppers and lettuce for a tossed salad, his watchful father warned him gently, 'Careful with that knife champ. Hold it how I showed you.'

Nick returned to marinating meat and prawns in a large glass bowl. Maggie's mind sank into fixed focus as she watched his big sensuous hands turning over the food. She shook herself free of the brief daze to peer into Christopher's steaming pot of chunky vegetables and watched in admiration as he ably stirred a thickening creamy sauce.

She inhaled deeply. 'Curry?'

He nodded.

Tyler was frying and flipping potato flap jacks on the stove like a professional, slopping huge spoonfuls of mixture directly onto the flat griddle and setting them on a large plate lined with baking paper when they were done before cooking the next batch. Presumably the bottle of tomato sauce on the kitchen table was ready to be splotched over everything before eating.

These guys all knew their way around a kitchen. Despite the small conflicts in any family, tonight the room was a hum of restrained male harmony. They accepted Maggie's presence without fuss. Of course, it could be they were all so busy in their tasks they barely noticed her arrival.

Nick washed his hands and asked her, 'Would you like your wine now?'

She nodded. 'That would be lovely.'

He opened the bottle and poured her a glass. 'Thank you. Are you sure there's nothing I can do?' She glanced about, unaccustomed to being idle.

'Sounds like you'll have your moment with that mystery dessert later.'

Nick snapped open a can of beer for himself and Maggie watched as he poured it into a handled glass tankard creating a perfect creamy foam on top.

'You've done that before.'

'A time or two.' He held out his drink and they clinked glasses.

'To neighbourhood cook ups,' she said.

'May there be many more.'

'Food for thought,' she quipped. Nick just groaned and shook his head.

Maggie wasn't sure quite how to interpret his

comment but she liked its promise. Apart from growing up, being part of a family as an adult was unfamiliar to her and she discovered it rewarding, making her even more determined to find one of her own.

Nick put his meats onto a tray and nodded in the direction of the side veranda. 'Want to come lend me moral support while I barbeque?'

She warmed at his invitation and followed him outdoors into the freshening early evening. The last rays of sun flashed through the bushland gum trees around his property perimeter. When Maggie returned her wandering gaze back to Nick, she stared at his chest and burst out laughing. He had tied on a full apron with the words *Women want me. Cows fear me.*

'Boys bought it for my fortieth a few years back,' he explained, grinning.

Maggie did quick maths. That made him anywhere from three to five years older than herself. She had figured him younger. Age sat well on Nick Logan.

For once, feeling comfortable with this family and her own growing inner contentment since leaving what she now realised was a crazy urban jungle, Maggie allowed the stillness to wrap around her. Even after only a matter of weeks into her new simple and quieter life in Tingara, she felt her strained city knots unwind and release.

'Penny for them,' Nick murmured.

'I was just thinking how at home I feel here in town already. A combination of many things but not least the friendliness of the locals.'

'It's a great little place,' Nick agreed, 'especially for kids growing up but it's not for everyone.'

Was he thinking of his ex-wife?

'What with driving and the boys, I don't socialise much.' He flashed her a quick glance. 'Mandy was a rare exception. We usually all go around to Will Bennett's place. We all fit better around his big old dining table. He married an English girl name of Hannah Charles who came on a house swap this past winter and clicked with him. He followed her back to England, proposed and they're currently travelling Europe.'

'That seems fast.'

Maggie reflected on her own swift connection with Leon that had turned out to be the biggest mistake of her life. She didn't plan to make another one. Any new man in her life that took her fancy would be admitted slowly and with caution.

Nick had paused before responding. 'Possibly but I guess they just . . . knew.'

When he sent her a soft challenging gaze, she reeled from its impact and the subtle message it conveyed. Those brown eyes reminded her of the rich earth she worked with daily. Difficult not to be fascinated by their depth and sincerity.

'Will and Hannah return soon from overseas for Mal and Emma's wedding. They're all great friends.' When he was done cooking, he began loading the food onto a plate. 'My work is done here,' he said and indicated for Maggie to go ahead of him as they returned indoors.

'All set boys?'

Serviettes and cutlery were piled in the centre

of the table. Each son proudly produced his own contribution to the meal.

'Maggie, if you'd care to sit here,' he pulled out a chair for her. 'Boys, sit anywhere and let's get this party started.'

She was touched by his gesture of respect to her gender and noticed he sat next to her at the head of the table. Noah positioned himself at her other side.

Maggie sniffed appreciatively. 'It all smells wonderful. This is so much fun. I'm a sucker for food, especially if someone else cooks it. I'm having a serve of everything.'

Food was handed around, plates piled high and a mouthful of food didn't stop the boys from talking while they ate. Mostly easy banter so the evening passed sociably. Maggie both sensed and caught Nick's eyes on her from time to time and everyone seemed cheerful, even Tyler, who dropped in wry one liners here and there. Noah chattered and Christopher just grinned and watched it all, saying little.

Replete and relaxed after the main course, Maggie said, 'I'll need to borrow your mixer now if that's okay.' She had already noticed it standing red and proud on the side bench.

'Wouldn't you know it's already plugged in and switched on,' Nick drawled.

'Dad did that for you,' Noah piped up.

'I suppose I did send out a hint,' Maggie confessed.

'Dad says no man should ignore a hint from a woman,' Tyler put in.

'They can brighten our lives,' Nick murmured,

embarrassed by his sons' honesty.

Then Noah piped up, 'Mummy didn't.'

All went quiet as silence dropped across the room.

Nick coughed and said quickly, 'She tried.'

While Nick and the boys cleared away, Maggie gathered up her bag of goodies and moved across to the mixer. She turned on the oven while she whipped fluffy egg whites for meringue and spread jam over the sponge cake.

'Mind if I use some ice cream?'

'Make yourself at home.'

Maggie dwelt on that comment as she retrieved a tub from the freezer, knowing she felt entirely comfortable here, and scooped out enough to cover the cake and jam, piled the meringue high on top to cover it on all sides and slid the tray into the hot oven.

She had an audience throughout the whole fascinating process until Noah cried out in alarm, 'You're putting ice cream in the oven!'

'It will soften a bit but it won't melt,' Maggie told him in reassurance, laying a hand on his shoulder as she explained. 'Dessert only takes five minutes and needs to be served as soon as it's done.'

She laid out a box of matches and a small bottle of brandy. When the timer beeped, she set the tray on a board on the table, drizzled brandy around its edges and struck a flame to the alcohol.

There were cries of *Whoa* and *Awesome* from the older boys, but a concerned wide eyed stare from Noah caused her to say wryly in reassurance, 'Unlike Minecraft, it doesn't blow up or anything.'

Noah sent her a relieved trusting grin.

Nick sat back, arms crossed, and said with lazy humour, 'Boys we're going to have to invite Maggie over here way more often.'

She loved cooking food and caring for people. She had been at Leon's beck and call too until he took advantage of her giving nature.

She shook off past memories and said, 'When my renovations are done it will be my pleasure to return the favour. Might be a bit of a squeeze around my small dining table though.'

'Sounds cosy.' Nick dropped a teaser and she glanced at him in surprise.

When the brandy flames burnt out, Maggie sliced a square of Bombe Alaska for everyone and no one spoke until each plate was scraped empty.

'Whoever invented this stuff is a genius.' Christopher made one of his rare comments.

'I believe its origins are either in Paris or New York,' Maggie said. 'Originally the ice cream was covered in pastry but nowadays we use meringue and it insulates the ice cream during the short browning time in the oven, so it doesn't really have time to melt.'

'Thank goodness for that,' Noah piped up quite seriously.

From habit, Maggie rose and began clearing plates.

Nick pushed back his chair, laid a big warm hand on her arm and said quickly, 'Not tonight, Maggie. You're our guest. Tyler, go clean the barbecue, please. Chris and Noah pack up all the leftover food into containers for the fridge.'

As the boys bustled about their allotted chores, Nick and Maggie stood companionably together at the sink, Maggie winning an argument to wash because he knew where to put everything away, so he happily grabbed a tea towel and dried.

Maggie noticed that after Tyler cleaned the barbeque, he went quiet and moved about the kitchen with his back to everyone then quietly stole outside. Nick either didn't notice or make much of it but by the time the kitchen was clean and set to rights again with Noah and Chris heading for the television to play Minecraft again, Tyler was still missing. Something was wrong. Maggie sensed it.

'Tyler be okay?' she ventured to Nick.

He nodded. 'He'll come back when he's ready.'

Clearly this had happened before. Maggie eyed the padded jacket over the back of the chair where Tyler had sat at the table during dinner.

She took it up and said to Nick, 'Getting cool out there. He might need this. Mind if I take it out to him?'

Nick scowled, insisting, 'He'll be fine.'

'All the same,' Maggie said gently with a shrug, 'just in case.'

Nick didn't look pleased and Maggie knew she was guilty of interference. Having felt so emotionally isolated in her own childhood through lack of self-esteem, especially the early teens, she was sensitive to young moods. For

Nick this might be a routine thing but men did tend to push their emotions aside. Tyler had issues and her heart went out to him.

Stepping outside to find Tyler, she didn't switch on a light. For some reason, Tyler was feeling vulnerable and the last thing anyone would want was to be exposed. She detected the boy's outline a short distance from the house and moved toward him. Tyler half turned at her approaching footsteps.

'Thought you might need this.'

She set down his jacket between them and perched on the other end of the log. Maggie's gaze drifted out across the half dark yard barely lit by a clouded moon and infinite stars.

'Gorgeous night. Be summer soon enough.'

Silence. When she risked a glance in his direction, Maggie noticed a glint of tears on his cheeks. This was really something for a boy of his age to show any feelings. She fished a clean pastel checked handkerchief out of her jeans pocket and handed it to him. Penny always teased her about always carrying one, said they were old fashioned and perhaps they were but at moments like this, they came in handy.

He took it, scrunching it up in his hands between his knees.

'Hope it's nothing I've done tonight?' she asked. He shook his head. 'Should I go get your Dad instead?'

'No!' Tyler said sharply.

'Listen, its hell keeping things in but I'm listening. Just saying.' She waited a moment before adding, 'I know I'm just a new neighbour

63

and you hardly know me but I hope we can be friends. Promise I won't judge or tell a soul. Sometimes talking is all we need.'

She waited patiently and they sat silently together. Voices travelled out to them from the kitchen. A dog barked somewhere in the neighbourhood.

'Is that *Lady*?'

'Nope.' Tyler sniffed and wiped his face.

Only the second word since she'd come outside. Progress?

'When I was out cleaning the barbeque,' he started quietly, 'I was thinking how much like a family we all were tonight.'

Quite an admission to a stranger. Maggie imagined where this had come from. Divorce was never easy especially for the children.

'You miss your Mum?'

'No! But I wish Dad hadn't married Rachel.'

Maggie winced. 'You've had this conversation with him before, I guess.' He nodded. 'Then you three precious boys wouldn't be here for your father now, would you?' she said quickly, noticing he didn't call her his mother. 'And families come in all shapes and sizes. Always have, always will. Even a shape we might not like.'

Difficult to measure how much of this the young man was absorbing or wanted to hear but she continued anyway.

'The past is done, Tyler. It doesn't do a lick of good dwelling on it. Nothing can change. We have to think about it, learn from it and decide how we'll live our lives or do things differently in the future.'

'Well I won't be getting married, that's for sure.'

'Be unfair to judge all women based on your experience with just one,' Maggie suggested.

'You didn't know her and you're not my mother,' he cried out angrily.

'No, I'm not, and I'm not trying to be or replace the one you already have.'

'She's not much of a mother anyways. She's never around.'

'Well I'd be powerful grateful if I was your mother,' she sighed.

'You wouldn't want me,' he muttered.

Maggie was surprised to hear this outwardly showy confident lad sounding so unworthy. 'Why ever not? Your tongue's a bit sharp,' she chuckled, 'but I love your sense of humour.'

She waited, hoping he might divulge some reason. Or not. When he didn't respond, she added, 'I'm not a mother but if you were my son-'

'Well you're not.'

'No and it's probably a good thing. Sounds like you wouldn't want me either.'

With the tables turned, Tyler shot her a narrowed glance. 'Why not?'

'Because I have no children and no hands on experience even though I have a niece and nephew I don't often see. Just because I want to be a mother doesn't mean I'd be any good at it. Good chance I'd be a failure. Especially with boys. Being a female myself if I had a daughter now I might have half a chance in knowing how to raise her.'

'They just raise their voice, yell a lot and slam doors.'

'I don't.' Maggie disagreed. 'Seems like we

have a similar problem. Men get *me* stumped. They go silent and disappear. Impossible to sort things out when that happens. I'm nearly forty and I still haven't figured out how to handle that.' Maggie shrugged. 'Females might argue but at least they talk.'

★  ★  ★

More silence. She considered how to break through yet not invade Tyler's personal space. Questioned even why she was bothering but there was something about this young man she couldn't set aside. She had probably already trespassed just by coming out here but at least he seemed receptive to listening. He could have got up and walked away.

★  ★  ★

'We all have a side of ourselves we don't like all that much,' Maggie continued, as though talking to herself, 'but everyone has some good in them. I know it's a personal question but can I ask what you liked about your mother?'

★  ★  ★

Tyler didn't hesitate. 'She was feminine, I guess, took care of her appearance. But she put herself first. Dad did a lot of stuff for her in the house. We had takeaways a lot when he was away on the road. She sure wasn't anything like you and didn't like to cook.' His joined hands hung

66

between his knees as he stared at the ground. 'It was nice having a lady in the kitchen again tonight. Like everyone's sharing and not being selfish.'

★　★　★

Not so surprising that the young were so perceptive. They watched and absorbed in reflection. Maggie realised Tyler had done that all night. Covered his lack of confidence with humour but growing up could be confusing and tough. You were no longer a child but not yet an adult.

★　★　★

'Well, thank you for the compliment. I feel privileged to be welcomed into such a neighbourly family. And I think a cook up is a brilliant idea. Not just everyone bringing a plate but everyone preparing it together. My mother is over seventy but even to this day you know she refuses to install a dishwasher in the kitchen. She says without it, standing at the sink washing and drying, two people generate conversation and there's nothing nicer.' Maggie sighed. 'I'm inclined to agree. Some of our best family chats were after a meal doing the dishes.' She paused. 'You feeling better?'

★　★　★

Tyler nodded and said a quiet and gruff, 'Yeah.' He paused, adding awkwardly, 'Thanks.'

67

'You're very welcome. And now,' she stood up and stretched, 'this old lady needs some rest. I'm heading home. By the way, great flap jacks. Night.'

# 5

Maggie heard Tyler's grunt in the dark and left him alone again. He was a decent kid and she felt sure he would be okay. It would just take time and patience and guidance.

Back inside, Nick tossed her a questioning glance and she smiled to let him know everything was okay. Sensing it was best to make a tactful escape, Maggie gathered up her carry bag and said goodnight to the younger boys. Surprisingly, Nick offered to walk her home.

'No need. I'm right next door.'

'Boys will be okay for five minutes.'

They were halfway across the cul-de-sac when Nick said, 'I overheard part of your conversation with Tyler.'

'Oh, I didn't mean to — '

'I talk to the boy but . . . ' he trailed off.

'I know. He said. He's just trying to be tough.'

'He's a softie underneath.'

'Like his father. Then he'll be fine.'

Nick chuckled in the dark as they walked and, despite a certain amount of tension, it stirred Maggie's heart.

'Judging by my own niece and nephew,' she said, 'seems kids grow up too soon. My parents are a quiet couple, not that sociable, homely, you know? But every now and again as we were growing up they just knew when something wasn't right with my brother or myself. Of course, they couldn't tell Paul a thing. He knew it all but for me a five minute conversation helped sort things out in my mind. They never preached. Just advised.'

In her driveway heading for the back door, Maggie said, 'Mal phoned and can start work on my new bathroom soon. I suggested that room first since it's the most desperate. Kitchen's workable. Just needs new cupboards. Then I'll get all new flooring and drapes or blinds.' She stopped, aware she was chattering, that Nick had turned silent and embarrassingly watchful. She grinned. 'Guess I'm boring you, huh?'

Then, despite their earlier strain, he made a move toward her. 'Thanks for everything you did tonight.' He dipped his head and fumbled a brief warm kiss that caught her off guard, then immediately apologised. 'Sorry, bit rusty.'

Maggie reeled back in surprise. Nick was an attractive kind man but she hadn't considered him romantically. Had she? He was a friend, right? Although she couldn't deny the odd fantasy about him *had* crossed her mind.

'What about Mandy?' she teased to cover her confusion.

'She made all the moves. Like I said, not my type.'

'Must have been others?' she probed.

'Rarely.'

'Nick, I like you but I'm recently solo myself — '

He softly placed a finger on her lips, still moist and tingling from his kiss. 'It's okay. I get it. These things take time.'

'We're neighbours,' she pointed out unnecessarily. 'If we don't work out, we have to live next door to each other. I just got here and I have plans. I'm not moving again.'

And there was something else important he didn't know about her that might discourage him. Best not to foster hope where none existed. Which was not to say she didn't find him appealing.

'And I've been here a good part of my life so I'm staying put myself. Friends for now?'

'Might be best.'

Which, in her opinion, left way too much open ended but she knew he liked her, enough to muster the courage when he felt the need to kiss her. If he hadn't pulled away so suddenly, she would have liked to follow it up with another but the first one left a positive impression. Even if they didn't plan to repeat it again any time soon. A sensible direction.

'Thanks for inviting me over. Cook ups are tops.'

They smiled wistfully at each other in the dark. As Maggie unlocked her door and heard Nick's footsteps crunching away on the gravelled driveway, she knew it was too soon to let any man into her life just yet. If ever. She had trust issues. She knew Nick more now but not all that well. She was attracted and tempted but was he too good to be true?

Nick Logan was a family man with kids. They were *his*. Not hers. The mother was estranged, the boys, especially Tyler, were still affected by the family break. Problem was, as much as she was growing captivated by Nick and attached to his sons, Maggie dearly wanted her own family. Not someone else's. Selfish she knew but there it was.

Spring made its presence ever more visible daily. To Maggie's delight, bulbs popped up everywhere in her garden. She marked out the areas and mentally designed the best landscaping and seasonal planting around them. Changed her original thinking and layout depending on what pushed up through the soil. Clearly Mrs. Black had once nurtured a wilderness garden but Maggie's vision while not formal would be more structured.

She saw Nick less. The thought occurred that he might just be busy or could be avoiding her because of the awkward kiss. Noah still trotted in occasionally but it was now school holidays. Nick and the boys had gone bush camping for a week.

Before they left Nick had called in to let her know they would be away and that *Lady* was with them.

'House and gates will be locked but I'd appreciate you keeping an eye on the place.'

They were still away. Maggie missed their comings and goings, the activity the family generated.

Nick's truck and motor bike were parked out the back of the house, the ute they had taken loaded with themselves, the dog and gear. It hadn't passed Maggie's notice that all Nick's vehicles gleamed. A man who took pride and care in his machinery.

Ironic that they had both been deserted by

their respective partners. Nick had openly mentioned that when it suited her, the boys' mother Rachel had them visit for the weekend. Apparently when she remarried, her older husband did not want kids around so sleepovers were rare.

Nick's house was untidy but happy and filled with loving chaos. To his credit, the man was raising his sons to be gentlemen. To be sure there would be challenging days and she had offered to help but they seemed self-sufficient.

Maggie hardly had time to reflect on her neighbour's absence. The monthly Tingara farmers' market took place in the central town park around its ornate rotunda. Although it was early days for Maggie's business and she seemed constantly weary from the unaccustomed physical work plus its resultant aches and pains, she took a small stall, mostly to promote her new nursery and hand out brochures. For the locals to get to know her.

The park buzzed with colour, locals and tourists and, for once, the showery days of late gave way at least for a few hours to the sunny brilliance of spring. As much as rain was welcomed by district farmers, vignerons and gardeners alike, Maggie's thoughts also went to Nick and the boys camping outdoors. She smiled to herself. Whereas she would worry, she was sure they were all loving the adventure. The whole Logan tribe seemed to need to burn off lots of male physical energy.

Between browsers at the market, Maggie's attention wandered around the park. The local

73

baker was selling his market loaf, a rustic crusty wholemeal bread only available on that day. Emma Hamilton had a jewellery stall. She caught Maggie's eye, waved and a short time later came over.

'Hi, Maggie. How are you settling into Tingara?'

'Really well. Busy. Meeting people.'

'My Gran, Mary, and even Ivy Ashford,' she said dryly, 'are so excited to hear it. You've brought a breath of fresh garden enthusiasm to town. We desperately need a decent nursery. When my fiancé, Mal, renovated his family's old homestead, *Clovelly*, across town, Ivy and Gran helped with ideas and advice in restoring its heritage garden.'

'Mal came to measure up my bathroom the other day. I'm so excited he can start work.'

'He loves the challenge and we need the money,' Emma laughed. 'Besides, you're Nick's neighbour and he put in a good word.'

'Really?' Maggie was touched that he had taken the trouble.

'Every spring in November locals open their gardens for charity. *Clovelly* will be open even though it has new owners now. Mal's boss actually. When your nursery is up and running, maybe next year, you might consider opening *Lakeside* for the weekend.'

'It's only a small cottage.'

'It's an historic property and people love them. And by then I'm sure your garden will be amazing. You should go down to the Information Centre and get them to stock your business

74

brochures. Stony Creek Way isn't exactly in the centre of town.' She smiled. 'You'll probably have local support mostly but you will catch some tourist trade of a weekend if you promote there. If you're interested.'

'Absolutely. Thanks for the suggestion.'

Emma ducked a glance toward her stall and hovering crowds. 'Must dash. Meet for coffee sometime?'

Maggie nodded and she was gone. Then, as if invoking her from the previous conversation with Emma, Ivy appeared with another woman. They stopped and she handed them each a brochure.

'You're Maggie Ellis, aren't you, dear?' the stranger asked and extended a hand. 'You've met Ivy I believe but I'm Mary Hamilton, Emma's gran.' She smiled broadly.

Unlike her companion, Mary stood neat and petite in tailored slacks and jumper with a scarf tossed in a colourful flourish about her neck and shoulders. Her wavy grey hair framed a sunny pleasant face.

'I'm pleased to meet you. Emma has spoken of you with much fondness. Morning, Ivy,' she acknowledged her friend hovering to one side.

Ivy mumbled something in response and Mary chuckled. 'She's unhappy because I made her close the shop.'

'Losing trade,' Ivy muttered.

Maggie marvelled that anyone could persuade Ivy to do anything against her will. Clearly a lifetime friendship hurdled that barrier.

'I'd love you both to drop by *Lakeside* any time. I could use any advice you might like to offer about my setup.'

Maggie hoped if she worded it that way, Ivy might be tempted to call. She might be blunt but she was honest and Maggie knew she needed that from people in her life these days.

'Spring's my busy time in the shop,' Ivy grumbled.

'We'd love to come.' Mary ignored her friend's excuse for Maggie suspected that's all it was. 'Haven't been in Mrs. Black's old cottage for years. She wasn't well in recent times. Kept to herself. In and out of hospital poor soul.'

Ivy glowered as the two elderly women moved on but Mary phoned Maggie within days and arranged to call, sending out a hint that Ivy loved chocolate cake. She obliged and waited anxiously for their morning arrival, actually needing and respecting Ivy's input. Soon Mary's little car hurtled into Maggie's driveway and she went out to greet them.

'I'll take you around the garden first then you can see what Mal's been doing inside while I make a cuppa.'

Ivy's attitude softened outdoors among the plants, identifying them all and making sharp comments on Maggie's ideas. Her mood lifted when Ivy appeared grumpily impressed as they entered her vast greenhouse.

'Going to be a bloody lot of work!' Ivy clicked her tongue and shook her head.

'It's all wonderful, dear,' Mary said with enthusiasm, nudging her friend. 'You're just green, Ivy, that you can't manage something like this anymore,' she teased. 'It's a relief to let the

76

young ones carry on now, isn't it?'

Her blunt devilish dig seemed not to offend her moody companion. The friends were total opposites in character but complemented each other, probably helped by knowing each other and living in Tingara all their lives.

Maggie felt for Ivy's longing looks and sharp critical gaze over the sprouting seeds, rows of planted out trays and organised potting bench; the mildness of the enclosure giving them respite from the morning chill. She hoped her fellow nurserywoman noticed some of her plant suggestions thriving already and Maggie's efforts in sourcing particular stock.

When she sensed they had lingered enough, Maggie said, 'Time for morning tea, I think. Come and have a look inside the cottage.' She led them indoors.

Mary rubbed her chilled hands as they entered. 'Lovely and cosy in here with the Aga. You've freshened up with light paint. I seem to remember dark walls,' she chuckled.

Ivy stayed silent but eyed off the chocolate Bundt cake dripping with icing and loaded with nuts on top sitting on a fancy china plate in the centre of the dining table.

'Go on down the hall to the bathroom while I boil the kettle. Mal's done an amazing job of gutting it all and retiling. All the fittings go in next weekend.'

Over a cuppa and more gardening conversation which actually flowed well and, despite her earlier prickly temperament, Ivy accepted a second slice of cake while Maggie enthused over

Mal and Daniel's two weekend visits that had achieved so much toward her renovations.

'While his father works, Daniel has been helping me in the greenhouse and buttering scones for snacks. My goodness that child is so like his father,' Maggie said, 'with those clear blue eyes and dark wavy hair. He's a very handsome boy. And when he flashes that cute dimpled grin, he could get away with anything.'

'He's a dear little man and another great grandson for me,' Mary beamed proudly.

'He was naturally wary of me at first but each visit he opens up more. Now he's discovered the outdoors he keeps himself busy for hours.'

Maggie's attention wandered as she contemplated all the children who had entered her life since moving to Tingara. She loved having the younger ones around in particular, perhaps because of their innocence and natural happiness, not to mention excitement over everything in the natural world.

Snapping herself from reflection, she continued, 'Mal says he'll only need two more weekends to fit out the bathroom and he's done. Then he can move into the kitchen.'

'He's a hard worker,' Mary agreed, adding proudly, 'Bagged himself a managerial position with Seth Duncan. The man travels the countryside buying up old derelict and neglected historic properties and restores them. Mal is one of his supervisors overseeing projects. He won the job when Seth bought that lovely old Webster homestead *Clovelly* and learnt Mal did all the restoration work. He was impressed and offered him a place on the Duncan team. He loves it.'

'He's certainly a master craftsman and pays amazing attention to detail. I'm so pleased with his work on my cottage here.'

Having remained silent and frowning, Ivy now stood up and said, 'Should be getting back to the shop.'

'No rush is there?' Mary said tactfully. 'Beth will stay and keep it open until you return. But I do agree we mustn't hold up Maggie any longer.'

They all rose and while Mary and Maggie chatted all the way out to the car, Ivy grunted a token goodbye and stalked away ahead of them to sit in it and wait.

'Nothing you've said,' Mary confided, reading Maggie's anxious glance. 'That's our Ivy. She's loved every minute of our visit. You saw her gaze of envy and admiration over every inch of your greenhouse. She might not be as active any more but she appreciates a keen fellow gardener. Take care of yourself, my dear.' Mary sent her a knowing look. 'You have a lot happening in your life at the moment, don't you?'

Maggie blanched in surprise at the observation. 'I'll manage,' she said brightly. 'It's all a challenge. I love what I'm doing and my new life in Tingara. Everyone has been so warm and inclusive.'

'If you ever need anything, just ask. I'd better move. I'm sure Ivy's edgy,' she chuckled.

After they left, Maggie wondered at Mary's comment. She couldn't possibly know, could she?

The following weekend Mal and a plumbing

mate arrived to install the bathroom fittings. She grew excited when Ted Peters from the hardware store had her units delivered during the week. The fabulous new bath had been a squeeze through the old narrow cottage doorways but with tweaking they finally managed.

The glass shower panel was installed and once the taps were connected, she would be good to go. Whether it was just having to cope and improvise around the bathroom renovation or the constant workload she set herself, Maggie had been feeling out of sorts in recent days. The dull ache in her back probably meant she had been overdoing lifting and stretching in the greenhouse. So it was a huge emotional boost to have half her indoor renovation almost complete.

She looked forward to long soaking and indulgent baths in her magnificent new tub soon. All things considered, she had hardly taken a moment to herself while organising her new life and business in Tingara but she determined to do so in the future.

Early the next week the Logans returned and it was barely hours later that Maggie heard little footsteps approach the greenhouse where she was working. She smiled to herself.

Without looking up, she said, 'I think I have a visitor.'

'It's me.'

'Hello me. How was your camping holiday?'

'Good,' he nodded. 'We did walking and fishing and stuff and we slept in a tent in sleeping bags. And we cooked on a campfire.'

'Sounds wonderful. Does Dad know you're here?'

Noah nodded. Maggie was pleased to hear it. She didn't want to overstep any neighbourly boundaries of their new casual friendship. With so much happening in their lives, it made sense. Although she had to admit missing Nick's easy company.

She had been standing for a couple of hours, moving between her potting bench and the pallets where she laid out endless rows of trays. So she wasn't terribly concerned when she felt a sharp stab of pain and caught her breath.

Noah's gaze snapped across to her when she doubled over. Maggie straightened again and smiled at the boy in reassurance.

'Think I've pulled a muscle,' she said.

A short time later it happened again. Concerned and sensing all was not well with her, Maggie said brightly and as kindly to Noah as she could, 'I think it might be time for lunch. Best pop home, okay? You can come back another day.'

'Okay,' he said reluctantly and she felt bad for sending the boy away.

As they walked from the greenhouse together, Maggie let out a sudden cry when her stomach clenched and she realised what was happening.

'Go home, Noah,' she said sharply. He hesitated, frowning. 'Now!'

'Are you okay?' he asked in a scared voice.

*No* she wanted to scream but instead she said. 'I'll be fine. I just need to rest.'

Her only concern was that Noah not witness anything of what she suspected was happening. Reluctantly, he wandered off along the driveway toward home, looking back as he went. She waved until he was out of sight then bolted for the laundry, feeling lousy and frightened. She stumbled indoors and dashed for the loo. Her heart and body screamed out in miserable realisation.

Maggie had no idea how much later but through her sobbing distress she gradually became aware of Nick's voice.

'Maggie?'

Her immediate thought was *Oh God, he can't see me like this*, yet deep down she frankly didn't care. Noah must have said something. She stayed silent, hoping he went away. She heard him knock on the back door and speak her name again then he was in the house calling from room to room. Until he was in the kitchen next door and it became inevitable that he would find her.

Shocked and shaking, she couldn't move. *He'll hate me.* She squeezed her eyes shut disbelieving any of this was really happening and Nick might somehow magically disappear.

And then he was hunkered down beside her. In every respect she was a mess.

'Maggie?' he said gently, resting a hand on her shoulder. 'What's the matter?'

Upset, she could only shake her head and she certainly couldn't face him.

'Noah came running home and said you were sick.'

Finally forcing herself to look across at him, she said softly with a catch in her voice, 'I've just miscarried.'

Nick groaned. 'Oh, Maggie, I'm so sorry.' And then, incredibly, he asked, 'Do you want me to call the father?'

She barked out an ironic laugh. 'I don't know who he is. IVF.'

'Ah.' He slid to the floor beside her and took her hand between his own.

The simple and warm physical contact and gesture was almost her undoing but, in this bare unlikely utility room with its random green walls and old linoleum flooring, Maggie found herself able to be honest and realistic with this man. Full of compassion, his company gave her strength.

'Please don't hate me,' she whispered. 'I didn't say anything because I was afraid of being judged.'

'I'm not judging you.'

Maggie reflected on his comment. Of course he wouldn't and she felt bad for mistrusting all men based on her own poor experience.

'I thought I did it for all the right reasons.' And then she blurted it all out. 'I wanted children, Leon didn't and then he dumped me. After I recovered from the shock, at first I panicked, thinking no one would ever want me again and I'd never have children. Then I got tough and decided I would solve that issue on my own. By donor sperm. At a fertility clinic.'

Maggie waited for Nick to say something but he remained still and silent, just listening. At least he hadn't run away yet. A hopeful sign. Her initial embarrassment in this devastating situation had turned to relief. She was now really grateful for his company and being able to confide in someone.

'After Leon and I broke up,' she continued, 'and at my age, I worried that I wouldn't ever have children. That I'd never be a mother. In recent years it's all I ever wanted.'

'There'll be another chance,' Nick said quietly, speaking for the first time since her announcement.

'Yeah, right. With who? By the time I meet a man and go through the dating and possible partnership thing, it could be years. I feel like I've been punished for my decision by some higher entity for daring to be a mother outside accepted norms.'

'It wasn't meant to be. Nature made the decision for you. There's no blame here. We're all hit with variables and sadness in our lives. I'm sorry you had to go through this Maggie.' She loved to hear him say her name. 'But,' he continued, 'you're an unbelievably attractive lady. A man would be proud to have you by his side. Wanting motherhood is an admirable and natural instinct for a woman.'

She knew that now and felt ashamed for thinking otherwise. 'Thank you. That means a lot.' She released a trembling sigh. 'I told my parents and they disapproved of what I did. They're strong believers in lifelong marriage even though I pointed out that couples these days don't necessarily marry or want a family.'

'Times change and society evolves and if they're unhappy, it makes sense couples don't stay married. In years gone by, women had less choice,' he added softly. He squeezed her hand. 'You may not think so now but you *will* become pregnant again if and when and how you want it. Rachel lost our first baby. For a long time that brought us closer together and she went on to give me three great sons.'

*Yes but you were already married*, Maggie wanted to scream. They sat together in silence.

'Want me to get you a cuppa?'

Maggie shook her head. 'No thanks. I think I'll go lie down and rest.'

'You be okay alone?'

She nodded. 'I'd prefer it.'

'Sure. I understand.'

Nick helped her stand, gave her a quick friendly hug and pressed a soft kiss to her forehead. 'You'll need support a while. I'll be around.'

The touch of his lips on her skin together with the smell and warmth and comfort from him made Maggie feel wonderfully safe and protected. How lucky was she landing a neighbour like this?

She slept, made herself a light evening snack and returned to bed for the night. Next day, she puddled indoors then forced herself to go out when the afternoon sunshine beckoned. She tilted back her head and closed her eyes, welcoming the rays over her body and using its soaking warmth to help heal her mind.

Despite feeling no excitement for work, Maggie staggered like a robot to the greenhouse, numb and only half alive. Nick was so convinced a child would happen again for her but, honestly, what were the odds? Her planning to achieve her dream as a single mum had been scary and exhilarating but a moving journey to do alone. Now, her heartbreak and utter sense of desolation at its failure was absolute.

She pushed herself to pot up and weed for a while but found only her hands were occupied because her mind strayed and she was hit by sadness. So she retreated indoors to feel miserable again, wondering when her unbidden bouts of weeping and emptiness would stop.

As if to mock her, the deepening October spring began to spread its colour and new life. White and pink blossom appeared everywhere, and huge rhododendron shrubs exploded into every shade from the softest pinks and mauves to vibrant crimson. Maggie witnessed but could not appreciate the seasonal show with the same pleasure as other springs and wondered if she would ever feel happy again.

# 6

Mal appeared on Saturday morning without Daniel this weekend for which Maggie was quietly grateful. Keeping company with his adorable son would only emphasise what she had lost. As her builder stepped into the cold kitchen, he seemed surprised to see her still in dressing gown and pyjamas when she was usually up and about, the aroma of something interesting usually already baking in the oven.

'Sorry,' she apologised, forcing a tepid smile. 'Feeling a bit weary this morning.'

'You're entitled I'm sure,' Mal said generously, 'what with working on your greenhouse and painting in here. A mate's coming shortly to help me install the bathroom fittings. That okay?'

Maggie nodded. 'Do what you must and ignore me. I'll get the fire going and boil the kettle. Maybe do a batch of pikelets.'

'Don't worry if you're not up to it today. We can nip down to the bakery for morning tea.'

'I'll take you up on that,' Maggie said, relieved, and started the Aga for warmth she hadn't realised both she and the cottage needed.

Once Mal's plumber mate arrived, banging and male voices carried out to her from the bathroom. Maggie was vaguely aware of their activity during the weekend but not fully invested in the beautiful room taking shape. Yet when Mal came to find her pottering in the greenhouse late on Sunday afternoon to tell her his work was done, she almost broke down and cried with gratitude.

Instead, she plastered a false brave smile on her face hoping it masked her apathy. When she followed him back indoors, the finished bathroom was revealed as a glorious, shining and white modern vision and she hugged Mal with heartfelt appreciation. But despite the room's magnificence and her most worthy effort, she still couldn't master full joy at the project's completion. She hoped Mal wasn't offended by her lack of enthusiasm. She only managed a deep sigh at another accomplishment to be ticked off her list in the transition to a new life in Tingara rather than the excited boost to her spirits she might have expected.

'You'll want to go shopping for that special mirror you want in here, I suppose?' Mal teased, clearly sensing her down mood.

'Eventually.' When she could gather the enthusiasm. At the moment she felt only a strong urge to withdraw from the world. 'No hurry. Perhaps next week.'

Apparently Maggie's indifference was more visible than she thought because next morning Emma arrived at her back door struggling under the weight of a large square and flat cardboard box.

'This is a lovely surprise,' Maggie said and meant it, uplifted by the bubbly friend's presence.

'I hope you don't think me presumptuous,' Emma wrinkled her nose, 'but I took a risk and bought this as a sort of cottage-warming gift. Mal showed me photos of his finished work and I thought this might work. He said you wanted something special.'

Maggie accepted the box, intrigued and touched. 'Thank you.' She began opening the ends to peek inside.

'Mal said you weren't feeling well over the weekend. You okay?'

Maggie stared at Emma and her timely arrival. 'Not really but I'll be fine,' was as much as she could admit.

'And Nick mentioned to Mal he's worried about you. Didn't say why.'

Maggie swallowed against that touching snippet of information bursting with happiness at the news that Nick cared enough about her to mention it to another bloke. 'Goodness that was so thoughtful.'

'Not working too hard, are you?' she smiled, glancing around. 'You're on your own here with loads to do.'

Maggie hesitated to confide in Emma, fearing a negative reaction as with Nick, but who else was available to share? Penny was in the city, hadn't known of her condition and now they hardly communicated. But Emma *was* becoming a trusted, if new, Tingara friend with whom she felt instantly comfortable. So Maggie took a deep breath and the whole story suddenly tumbled out, at the end of which Emma grabbed her for a long meaningful hug.

'You know,' Maggie said as she unashamedly wiped away yet more tears, 'Nick sat with me on

89

the laundry floor while I looked and felt horrible and just held my hands. For ages. In silence. It was all I needed and he seemed to sense it. Then he told me Rachel lost their first baby.'

Emma raised her eyebrows. 'Really? I didn't know.' She frowned. 'I have heard miscarriages are more common than we realise. Plus women are having families later in their lives for many reasons. My sister, Julie in Sydney, lost two babies between her older child Zach and daughter Mia. She's very pregnant again now and all's well so far. Fingers crossed. Now you sit down,' she pointed to a dining chair, 'and I'll put the kettle on. Gran says a cuppa and chat fixes anything. I've heard you're a great cook. Please tell me you have cake.'

Maggie couldn't suppress a grin. 'In the pantry. Ginger.'

'Yum.' She found it and cut slices then opened the fridge and read the label on a tub. 'Double cream. Awesome. A fellow sinner. This stuff is absolutely essential with a slice of Will Bennett's legendary apple cakes. You wait till you try one when he and Hannah get back, our wedding is over and we all have our regular social dinners together again. They're due back from Europe any day now.'

Emma paused in reflection, shaking her head. 'I can't believe Hannah has left England to settle in Tingara with Will. Mrs. Bennett.' She grinned. 'We all thought he was a confirmed bachelor. Sexy quiet type our Will. Needed a special woman to complement him. Hannah's gorgeous. Long blonde hair, blue eyes. True English rose.

But beneath that soft exterior is a clever accountant and clearly one firm woman because she landed Will. Although you could see it was mutual. Maybe Will landed Hannah.' Emma laughed. 'Either way, we're all delighted for them both.'

Emma's gentle gossip, her female company, the way she easily and casually took charge, and the relief of her own disclosure had a soothing effect on Maggie. The warmth from this cheerful friendly person made the first advance into her private anguish.

When they finished eating and chatting, although Maggie had mostly been content to listen, her attention focused on the box gift again.

'I must open your parcel.'

By the time she had struggled with tape and flaps, withdrew the item and ripped off its bubble wrap, Maggie felt a stirring of interest.

'Oh it's beautiful,' she gasped.

'Not too bright?'

'No! It's wonderful.'

In her hands, she held a square mirror with a glittering mosaic border in just enough jewel colours she knew would enhance her bathroom.

'Mal put up a hook for me. Let's go hang it.'

Its size and design proved perfect for the small room.

Emma left soon after but not before clearing away their tea things and rinsing the dishes in the sink. Maggie was touched by the womanly gesture.

'Take care of you,' Emma hinted, hugged her

goodbye and waved.

Maggie knew she had made a lifelong friend.

The following days grew easier. Each night Maggie lit fat candles, turned off the light and indulged in a soothing bath. She slept better and slowly looked forward to a fresh morning, returning to her routine in the greenhouse.

Mid-week, she had just barrowed another load of compost as late afternoon shadows lengthened across her garden when Nick and the boys walked up her driveway, Noah carrying a bundle of something that completely filled his tiny arms.

'I hope you're all feeling strong,' she joked, leaning on her shovel.

'Tyler?' Nick said.

The boy looked unusually willing. 'Are you sure?' she asked, unsure after their D and M following the cook up the other week that she was in favour with him. He nodded so she said, 'Great. All this lot needs to be shovelled into my potting bin.'

After she showed him where, an uncomplaining Tyler took up the spade and set to work. Maggie and Nick shared a meaningful gaze and she smiled to reassure him.

'Emma called in,' she said simply, presuming he would understand since his concern for her welfare had prompted the visit. *Thank you*, she mouthed. 'She brought me a gift for my new bathroom,' she added more loudly again. 'Want to see it?'

The bundle in Noah's arms moved and he sent a pleading glance up to his father. 'Can we give her this first?'

'What's this about?' she looked between them all.

'I told Dad you weren't feeling well so we wanted to cheer you up,' he said proudly, grinning, extending the bundle toward her.

Maggie had her suspicions so when she drew open the folds of the old blanket wrapped around their surprise, she discovered the sweetest fluffy face of a ginger kitten. She understood its significance. A creature to love.

'For me?' Noah's small head nodded madly as she accepted it with humble gratitude and pleasure, making a huge effort in front of the boys to withhold tears. 'He or she is adorable.'

'She,' Noah said eagerly. 'Dad said you'd probably want a female in the house with all us men for neighbours.'

Maggie laughed and felt the first stirrings of happiness in a while. 'She will be a treasured companion. It was very thoughtful of you all. I'm feeling much better.'

When Noah gave her a random hug around the waist because that was as high as he could reach, Maggie was almost undone again but held it together.

Standing aside quietly beside his father, Christopher said, 'You'll have to give her a name.'

'Yes I will.' She thought a moment but already knew. Her father's two older spinster sisters had been ardent gardeners during their lifetime, encouraging Maggie, and influenced her similar interest in childhood. Had she been gifted a daughter — emotion caught in her throat at the

93

futile thought — she would have named her Milly Grace after them both.

Maggie supplied an abridged version to her visitors. 'Milly.'

Noah beamed.

Nick remained disturbingly observant but now looked over Maggie's shoulder. 'You all done, Tyler?'

'Yep.'

'Thank you. Any time you want to earn some pocket money . . . ' she teased.

'Boys, go on ahead and clean up before dinner,' Nick said. He turned and waited until the trio had ambled far enough along the driveway to be out of hearing before he added, 'You okay?'

'Getting there. Emma's visit yesterday helped enormously and the kitten will play a part in helping, too, I'm sure.' She smiled down at the warm cute bundle in her arms.

Impulsively, because he was standing there so close and looking too damned handsome and she had come to rely on his company, she stood on tiptoe and kissed his rough cheek. 'Thank you for Milly. I'm really touched.'

'You're very welcome,' he drawled. 'Haven't bothered you about staying with the boys.'

'Sorry about that but I'm feeling better,' she brightened. 'I need to get about again. It's just a confidence thing, really.'

'Don't push yourself. When you're ready. I'm taking short haul jobs and I've had yet another chat with Zoe. Explained the importance of being reliable and that I need to be able to trust her with the care of my sons. She didn't like to hear it but I told her to be careful with Jake.' Nick looked down at her softly. 'You take care now.'

Maggie nodded, seeing his struggle to keep his hands in his pockets and blessed him for not giving in. She wasn't ready yet. She needed more time but, all things considered, she owed it to herself not to ignore this man for too much longer, didn't she? Sadly, she was free now in every respect. Against her will on both counts. Making her realise the fragility of the ticking clock of time and life and that she must not squander a single moment.

Even after only a few days, Maggie had missed this quiet giant of a friend and generous warm hearted family man. She resigned herself to the fact that there would always be this stirring inside her when he was around. A tension that was never quite resolved. They both sensed its presence but currently denied it. If their mutual spark was ever pursued she knew exactly what would happen and fiercely resisted not only the idea but the reality should it eventuate.

It occurred to Maggie that her growing feelings for Nick always surfaced regardless and overrode her recent physical and emotional upheaval. That Nick had played a part in it seemed ironic and yet logical for, as neighbours, he was destined to be in her life now anyway.

Nick hesitated but eventually murmured, 'Night,' and walked away, his muscled body moving easily in jeans with each long stride, arms swinging at his sides. Easy on the eye for sure, she sighed, questioning if and where their friendship might lead.

Maggie shook her thoughts free, her heart melting at the kitty bundle she held. 'You're going to need food and your own bed so I need to go shopping.'

The distraction she needed. Locking her tiny new housemate in the laundry and hardening her soft heart to ignore its appealing mews, Maggie drove into town feeling strangely peaceful of heart.

Luke greeted her brightly as she entered the hardware store, buzzing with customers. Tourists, she noticed, not only locals. Was it the weekend? She frowned. Yes, Saturday. How could she not have known? Because of her mental haze in recent days of course during which she had simply lost track of time and the world around her.

Maggie returned Luke's smile. 'I need kitten food, litter and your most comfortable basket.'

'Ah, we've acquired a pet.'

After she had loaded Milly's supplies into her vehicle, Maggie settled on another decision in helping her to move on with her life and, a few doors down on the same block, crossed the threshold into Ivy's shop, redolent with the damp earthy smells of nature. Because Ivy was busy serving a customer, Maggie strolled out the back to the undercover area, heading for rose bushes and reading labels for the most fragrant. She took it back inside and waited at the counter until Ivy was free. The poor soul looked weary and Maggie was tempted to offer assistance but guessed it might be met with indignation by the proud woman. Some people were difficult to help.

'Should be planted in winter,' Ivy nodded to Maggie's chosen rose.

'Yes it should but I'm sure it will survive.' Maggie handed over cash and while Ivy fumbled in the outdated manual till, she added, 'My seed trays are all sprouting so I should have my first batch of seedlings ready for you soon.'

'Good. I need them,' she muttered.

Maggie hid a smile. 'I hope it will be more convenient for you buying locally. I appreciate your support. I'll by supplying Ted, too.'

Ivy grunted, finally handed over Maggie's change and moved on to another customer without a word.

Dusk found Maggie digging a hole in her rear garden. Since feeling more settled and making new friends in Tingara, her recent grief, she noticed, still raw but gradually easing. She knew she was here to stay long term so she planted her fragrant rose bush in remembrance. Every time she passed, and especially when it flowered, its perfume would rise to her senses, she would remember and smile.

'For you, my little one,' she whispered as she levelled the last shovel of dirt, thinking of more than one baby.

With each new day and development in her life, Maggie tried to regard her lost child as a hopeful experience. She knew she could get pregnant and carry a baby. One day she might again. But whatever happened in the future — and who could see or know — the tiny lost soul would never be forgotten.

That night, as Maggie lit her candles as usual for her bath, she sent up a silent prayer.

The following week with Milly snuggled on her lap while Maggie opened the mail during a lunch break, she was excited to unfold an invitation to Emma and Mal's wedding.

It sat proudly on her mantelpiece above the Aga causing food for thought firstly over what to wear. A new outfit? And secondly, the gift. She noticed Ted's hardware was suggested as a registry so that decision was easier and sorted. A spring dress was another matter. Maggie wanted to be feminine and appealing for no doubt Nick would be there and, wisely or not, she wanted his approval. Her *plus one* wouldn't apply.

She considered taking a few days off to go down to the city and shop. It would be an ideal chance to catch up with Penny and reconnect. Their exchanged phone calls had grown shorter and further apart which shocked Maggie. Their strong bond appeared to be slipping. Partly her fault she knew, feeling guilty, being so busy setting up her business; not making time and neglecting their long friendship. On the other hand, Maggie's open invitation for Penny to visit was never taken up either.

In the end the following week, while browsing in every dress shop in town, of all places Maggie finally found a dusky pink vintage dress she loved, its hem trimmed with a wide band of lovely delicate old lace. Mary helped her find it when she called in to buy fresh farm eggs among other local produce sold in the op shop.

'With your lovely auburn hair, that colour

suits you perfectly, dear.'

'You think?' Maggie wasn't sure and dithered, turning this way and that. Had her figure slimmed with all the physical work of recent weeks?

'Positive. Do you have pearls?' Maggie nodded. 'Then you're done.' Mary beamed.

'What's the grandmother of the bride wearing?'

Mary chuckled. 'I'm not falling for that one. You can wait and find out like everyone else. The evenings are still cool. Do you have a shawl?'

'Yes, an ivory lace one a friend brought me back from Asia.'

Penny had gone alone and not invited Maggie but then that was the early days soon after meeting Leon and she had been thoroughly wrapped up in him. At odd moments, even after more than a year, his memory still stung but those times were growing less.

After breakfast one morning, Maggie had actually taken a day away from the greenhouse and was covering up the ghastly green paint in the laundry with a paint roller. As she stood on the top step of her house ladder with the door open to let the fumes escape, Nick appeared in the space.

'Should you be doing that?' he scowled.

'Of course, it's my house.'

'I mean-'

'I know what you mean. I'm not an invalid. I'm fine.' Her short reply rattled him for a moment but he took it in his stride. She took a deep breath and descended the ladder, tempering her words. 'Thanks for your concern but there's no need to fuss. Really.'

'I care,' he said softly.

*And so do I.* The truth made her sigh. 'And I appreciate it. But if you could think of me normally that would help.'

'Sure.'

'How are the boys?'

'Fine. I'm doing the school run shortly.'

He cleared his throat and ran a hand through his hair. He's nervous. Why? Maggie rinsed her roller in the trough and turned for the kitchen. 'Guess you don't have time for a cuppa.'

He shook his head and checked his watch. 'Best not.'

'At least sit down a minute.'

He sat opposite her at the dining table, folding his hands but hesitating to speak his mind. Meanwhile Milly leapt onto her lap and Maggie stroked her.

'Boys are with their mother this weekend. Thought you might appreciate a day out and a break from your garden. Do something together, you know?'

'You mean like a date?' she ventured.

Nick shrugged. 'Just a casual outing together really. Nothing in it.'

'Ah. Of course.'

Maggie stifled a grin and a burst of excitement whipped through her chest. Nick Logan was embarrassed to be asking. His discomfort was so sweet, especially coming from such a blokey bloke. It *was* a date and he couldn't deny it. She was stoked. And scared, but she would do this and see what he had in mind.

Point was, considering the feeler he was

sending out, if she accepted, her agreement would signal a willingness to go out with him, be with him, and where would that lead? By showing interest, Maggie was not only getting involved with Nick but also his family.

It was a no brainer. She knew the answer without having to think about it. Depending on the outcome, what she needed to give deeper thought was *what happens next?* She was a sucker for a warm hearted guy. Leon had been. At first. But he eventually proved selfish. Nick wasn't. He was totally the opposite, making her rethink her stance on men.

Because of her mature figure, she tended to feel flattered when a man showed interest. Not such a common event in her life in the past so she had been inclined to tumble into a relationship after only a glance in her direction.

Nick was staring at her nervously. 'Maggie?'

She shook herself back into the moment. 'Um . . . yes. That might be nice. As you say, a break from work, nothing more. Just thinking what day might be best. For both of us.'

When Nick beamed at her response, Maggie mentally crossed everything and hoped it was the right choice. That the word *regret* didn't come back to bite her at some point in the future.

'Any ideas?'

'I haven't had a chance to explore the area much. A drive might be nice?' *Nice?* Maggie cringed. So lame.

Her suggestion seemed to delight him. 'A ramble it is, then. Sunday morning? Head out before lunch and grab a bite to eat?'

Maggie nodded. Sounded harmless enough. A drive in the country and a meal in a cafe or pub somewhere among other people should be doable and not too intimate.

'Jeans and comfy shoes, in case we do some walking?' Nick suggested.

'Sure. Makes sense.'

Maggie thought it odd that he would suggest what to wear but maybe he was just making sure they both dressed casual and kept their outing the same. No pressure. Just an easy day together. Although he did tend to eye her off with appreciation no matter what she wore. So after Nick left, she set his comment to the back of her mind.

# 7

By Saturday evening, Maggie had finished painting the laundry. Mal was due to return next weekend to measure up her kitchen for new cupboards. She had protested he couldn't possibly have time this close to the wedding but he brushed her objections aside.

With the greenhouse up and running, producing plants and therefore an income, and the minor cottage renovations almost done, Maggie felt the burden of establishing her new life in Tingara slowly easing.

So she looked forward, cautiously, to her date with Nick. He had held her hands and tried a token kiss which she had spoiled by rejection but could there be more between them? She guessed today was one way to find out.

On Sunday morning as Maggie finished dressing, she heard a loud engine rumbling outside. Who on earth was invading their cul-de-sac? They usually didn't get much through traffic.

Maggie twitched aside the new lace curtain at her bedroom window and gaped. An edgy guy in tight jeans and a black leather jacket was easing one leg over a shiny motor bike to dismount. When he removed his helmet, Maggie's alarm was confirmed. Nick! Their outing was going to be on *that*? They would freeze and also need to get very very close. Like pressed-up-against-each-other close. A passenger needed to cling on

103

tight when you rode one of those contraptions. Especially Maggie since she'd never been on one before.

Suddenly she twigged to Nick's clothes suggestion. She had hardly touched the man let alone wrap her arms around his waist. Which is exactly what she would need to do to stay on. A fleeting thought crossed her mind to back out but although Maggie might be a pushover sometimes, she had never considered herself a coward. Think positively. This would be an experience, right?

Nick was knocking on her newly painted bright red front door. She gave herself one quick last glance in the mirror then grabbed a rain-proof coat and a thick woollen scarf because she sure was going to need it.

Nick ogled her as she emerged from the cottage and accompanied his cheeky smile with a wink.

'Jeans and solid shoes for walking, huh?' She pulled a wry face.

'We could do that later,' he said easily.

'Now why would we bother when we have such an exciting machine to take us places instead?' she teased.

Nick stepped aside as she closed the door and indicated the two shiny wheels in her gravelled driveway. 'I'd like you to meet *Betsy*.' Maggie must not have hidden all her doubts because he added reassuringly. 'It'll be fun.'

'I can see I'll have to hold on really tight.'

'Absolutely.'

Which was your intention all along, Maggie

thought, realising she was being soaked up in his deeply personal gaze and that so much more sexy devilment brewed beneath the surface of this attractive man. So much for just being neighbours.

'What's first?'

Nick handed her another helmet. Maggie settled it on her head. So much for all that wasted effort washing and styling her hair which was crammed underneath it. He gently brushed aside her nervous fumbling fingers with his own to adjust the strap beneath her chin and closed the visor.

'After I'm on, leg over onto the rear seat, feet onto the rests,' he pointed out, 'then shuffle forward and grab me tight, okay?'

His lazy grin melted her heart. She intended to appreciate this man in her life wherever their friendship led and throw herself fully into the day. So long as she clung on tight, although daunted, Maggie was positive she would be fine. Challenges like this broadened your horizon and would surely boost her confidence.

Nodding, she asked, 'Where are we going?'

Nick shrugged. 'No idea. Any requests?'

He hadn't planned anything! They were winging it? 'You know the area better than I do. Surprise me. More than you already have today,' she chuckled.

He tugged his own helmet back on, flipped down the visor and mounted his beast of a machine. She followed his lead and sat behind.

He half turned to speak. 'We'll take it slow for a while, okay?'

The bike or this crazy thing that was developing between them she wondered? Then he flicked *Betsy* into life and they were away.

O. M. G.

They weren't ten minutes down the road and the smile plastered on Maggie's face simply would not disappear. She knew because she had been trying to wipe it off for kilometres.

'This is awesome,' Maggie leaned forward and shouted to the back of Nick's helmet.

He gave her a thumbs up to let her know he heard. It was scary to be so exposed on this thing. *Betsy*, she reminded herself, but Nick had been true to his word and they were thundering along country roads at a leisurely pace.

Amazing how much more scenery one noticed and how clearly as they rumbled along. Nick's back was broad and solid and comforting. She had shyly found a hold by sliding her arms under his soft leather jacket and linking her hands low across his chest. He was warm pressed up against her but despite feeling self-conscious at first, Maggie was slowly loosening up and thrilling to the whole adventure.

After half an hour, they stopped at a roadside stall, removed their helmets and stretched their legs. From an honesty box of produce, Nick grabbed and paid for mandarins and a small box of homemade sugar biscuits.

As they snacked, Nick asked, 'How you travelling?' leaning against a fence post and crossing his legs encased in tight black jeans with a wide leather cowboy belt. All man, she sighed with pleasure, admiring the view. No checked

106

shirt today. A tight tee shirt on a body like that was actually quite a turn on.

'I can see how you might become addicted,' she confessed.

'It's freedom and good for the soul.'

'I'd have to agree.'

They hung over the fence together gazing out across a small vineyard its neat rows of vines clinging to a slight incline leading down into a valley.

'You can tell the variety of grape by its leaf.'

Nick chuckled. 'Good to know I guess but I drink beer.'

'One of the few worthwhile facts Leon taught me.'

On impulse, she ducked between the fence wires and sprinted across to the nearest vines to pluck some large heart shaped leaves. She returned to a grinning Nick who was shaking his head as he held the wires apart so she could squeeze through and scramble back onto his side.

'Thank you,' she bowed, laughing, feeling light and free and on the verge of a true happiness she hadn't known in years.

'You're not just a gorgeous face,' he drawled, 'but I already knew that.'

'Focus,' she teased back. 'See this leaf?' She held it up. 'Each one has its own design. This main lobe part, the edges or fingers and holes, and the surface.' She assessed it for a moment. 'Because this one has a smooth surface with lots of crinkly edges I'd guess its sav blanc. Not my favourite wine. I prefer a rosé but still a good drop.'

'High country around here has lots of small wine regions. Lots of Italian varieties in the King Valley apparently.'

'Must try some.'

She licked her lips and not just over the thought of wine. Nick was looking really hot standing with hands on hips, and that fitted tee shirt stretched across his chest. A moment of recognition passed between them. Nick broke it first but not before Maggie noticed his gaze narrow and jaw clench as he turned to stow their leftovers in the rear saddlebag.

When they mounted the bike to get back on the road again, in Maggie's mind it was with a whole new awareness of the other person. Even through layers of clothing, her breasts tingled as they pressed up against him, her arms clenched around his girth and that soft leather jacket.

The throaty engine throbbed into life, the tyres spat dirt as he zipped away, his daredevil stunt action like a dare and a promise. Maggie was up for it and loved the idea of his implied challenge. A new perception had entered her thinking today.

For the next hour, Nick led them on a feast of exploration through the district. They spun through the dappled shadows of woodlands, leant into corners together, Maggie long since having grown accustomed to the quirks of riding passenger behind a gorgeous man on a motor bike.

God she hoped he asked her out again. This was the best day.

From being surrounded by trees, they would

burst out across open grassy countryside dotted with sentinel eucalypts, neat lines of vineyards or grazing cattle and frolicking horses. They crossed small rustic bridges over the clear rushing waters of creeks meandering down from the soft rolling hills beyond.

The scenery unfolded around them, the chilly air adding to the cosiness of being hugged together on the bike as they breezed along.

Exhilarated when Nick stopped at a small village pub for a late lunch, Maggie dismounted, removed her helmet and shook her hair free. She stretched, catching Nick watching her.

'All good?' he murmured.

'Very happy.'

They shared a stupid mutual grin then went inside to indulge in a long lazy roast lunch and even longer conversation. Maggie was feeling way too comfortable with Nick, probably affected already by the fact he had been around for her at the worst time of her life when she needed someone most.

'You wanna talk about anything, I'm here,' he suggested at one point.

Maggie understood what he meant. They had shared something deeply personal in common that would always be a bond for them.

'Tell me about *your* family.'

'Coward,' he teased softly. 'I asked about you.'

'Well I turned the tables. Go for it.'

'Guess it all started with my parents,' he winked. 'Charlie and Liz. We had a tough family. I'm one of seven brothers and sisters who all grew up in country Queensland. Folks are still there but my brothers and sisters are scattered all over Australia. We keep in touch but don't get together as a family much.

'My parents are working class, always struggled. My old man mistreated my mother. My brothers and I protected her as much as we could. We confronted Dad but it made no difference to him. He never changed. Great pity for our mother but she stayed. So us kids got out as soon as we could. I vowed when I married I would treat my woman right.'

As Nick talked and Maggie watched the play of emotions cross his face from fond nostalgia to gritty determination, she could see he had come a long way alone. From a broken marriage to turning himself and his sons into the best family he could make in the circumstances.

'I overdid it with Rachel though. Treated her like a goddess. Spoilt her I guess until everything I did for her or bought for her wasn't good enough anymore. She only had to ask and I would get it for her. My mistake. I could see she was unhappy, unsettled, and it turned my guts inside out. Nothing I did could change it. I knew she wouldn't stay. Could see the writing on the wall. When she remarried her rich sugar daddy,' he said sadly, 'the guy didn't want kids around so I gladly accepted sole custody. Rachel was happy to let her sons go.'

The truth of voluntarily and selfishly giving up your own children for who you were morally responsible, when there was no genuine need, hit Maggie like a blast. Her outrage screamed inside. What she wouldn't give for three beautiful healthy children of her own. Her heart clenched and a shot of pain cut through her to be reminded of her recent loss and another one all those years ago. She would die before she would give up a child.

Even through her private heartbreak, Maggie reached across to Nick and rested a hand on his arm. 'Her loss, your gain.'

'That's how I see it, too.'

His gaze turned distant out through a nearby window and onto the quiet small town street. When he looked back again it seemed he had banished memories and cleared his mind.

'Your turn.'

Maggie sighed. 'Fair enough. All my family live in Melbourne, out east. My parents are Mike and Carol. My only brother Paul is married to Debbie with three children, Melissa, Skye and Dean. They're all at school now. Debbie popped them out, bottle fed them for six months then put them in child care. After both she and Paul work all week, weekends for them are endlessly cleaning, gardening and socialising. I get exhausted just thinking about it. They either don't have or make much time for the kids. Everything has to be luxury. Grand two storey house as perfect as a display home, name brands, cars, designer clothes, lavish catered parties. Debbie doesn't cook. What kind of family is that? I'd rather have none than let someone else raise my children. What's the point of having them in the first place?'

'They sound miserable trying to maintain standards.'

'We have nothing in common,' Maggie said sadly. 'By comparison, I'm so basic, love getting my hands dirty, and would love a tribe of kids crawling all over me. I can live with a little dust on my furniture. I prefer this simple quiet life in the country over the city any day now. Didn't realise how much until I moved to Tingara. I can't compete with perfection and I don't even try.

'Paul and I were raised in an ordinary family home with love but for my big brother nothing was ever good enough. He always wanted more. When he met Debbie, his demands escalated. They strove and competed together. Both say they can't afford not to be working but I doubt they're happy. Stressed more likely and on that roundabout lifestyle they can't get off. Mum and Dad help out far more than they should. I, on the other hand, was always expected to manage by myself.

'Then for the decade I was Leon's partner, I hinted and hoped for children but it fell on deaf ears. Now, especially after recent events,' she said carefully, darting him a quick glance, 'I need to accept I'm unlikely to ever be a mother.'

She stopped to catch her breath. 'It hurts. I could weep every time the thought crosses my mind. By now I expected to be married and raising my own family, not thousands of seedlings,' she said wryly and pushed out a long frustrated sigh. 'My plants will be my babies to tend and I'd love to teach children the joy of gardening.'

'You should approach the local school. Get them to help work in your garden for a lesson and the experience. My boys love any excuse to get outdoors.' He paused. 'Being a city woman, is the country living up to your expectations?'

'Absolutely,' she enthused. 'My business is almost up and running, my cottage is almost finished and I've met wonderful neighbours and friends. I chose Tingara because of the climate. It's ideal for gardens, tourist trade is a bonus and I love the peace. Once I decided on the place, I let my fingers do the walking and researched real estate on my iPad, chewing up my monthly mobile phone budget making endless calls to Anne Perry. When she showed me *Lakeside* I knew I'd found my dream property. The cottage is compact but that's not a problem. I'm nudging middle age and probably destined to stay single so it's more than enough for my needs and business. 'Tell me,' she dared to ask, 'do the townsfolk talk about me? You know, single woman, no man, no kids, no life?'

'I've only heard positive comments about you. Your present situation isn't entirely of your own making though, is it?'

'No.' There was that twinge of hurtful envy again rearing up. Maggie added over brightly. 'What is it to me that my ex prefers a leggy olive skinned Italian siren like Natalia still in her twenties and utterly gorgeous with long glossy black hair trailing down her back and superb breasts that only just manage to stay inside her clingy clothes? I hope she's using birth control,' she muttered, 'because Leon doesn't want kids. Sorry,' she cringed. 'Poor taste slamming my ex. I'm above that.'

'It's okay to vent.'

'I didn't intend to spoil our day.'

'You haven't.' He considered her a moment. 'What's next for you?'

Maggie shrugged. 'It's daunting to think I might grow old alone.'

'Can't see that happening.'

'You know something I don't?' she chuckled. Nick shrugged and stayed silent so she went on, 'I had two elderly maiden spinster aunts, Grace and Millicent, aunt Milly.'

'The kitten?'

She nodded. 'My father's older sisters who lived in the Ellis family home together all their lives after my grandparents died. They were lifelong companions but as they aged they had no voice of their own and were told what to do. The family talked past them as if they weren't in the same room and made the decision for them to move out and sell up to settle in aged care. My heart broke for them. I don't want that for me,' Maggie announced with determination.

'But the fact is I have to start over again after wasting some damn precious years of my life on a man who kept promising but didn't deliver.'

'You're not alone.' Nick covered her with a meaningful soft glance.

'No, you're right. I should be more positive and grateful.'

They had talked long enough after the meal for Nick to have a mug of hot chocolate and Maggie a pot of tea but they were finished now.

'Ready to move on?'

Once more Maggie snuggled up against Nick's

back and let him choose their destinations. Turned out it was two small towns where they stretched their legs and browsed antique shops. On their last roadside stop, Nick fired the bike up a winding hill to a lookout and waterfall cascading below.

Maggie shook out her thick hair and combed fingers through, walking ahead of Nick on a ferny bush trail with a creek gurgling over stones beside them. The path was rocky in places so it seemed natural when Maggie stumbled that Nick reached out and clasped her hand. Somehow he never let go and linked their fingers. An unspoken warmth flowed within her and hung between them in the nippy afternoon of late spring, cooler up here in the hills.

It was a wrench when they returned to the bike in the car park and Nick let her go.

'Head for home?' his voice was soft and husky as they stood close, bodies brushed together.

His half smile was laced with meaning and she would not have been at all surprised if he had kissed her. It was that intense. Maggie merely nodded, speechless, confused by her emotions and was turning toward the bike when Nick clearly had second thoughts, too, because he grabbed the ends of her scarf and tugged her back.

Help! Maggie was totally not ready for this but Nick planted a full and warm lingering kiss on her mouth. Her eyes naturally closed while she savoured the lush feel of his lips on hers and strong arms wrapped around her.

When it ended and they drew apart, he

drawled, 'Thanks for being a good sport and trusting me.'

'You're welcome.'

'Rachel never got on the back of my wheels with me,' he admitted as they drew apart.

Maggie eyed him steadily. 'She'll never know what she missed.'

'And what would that be?' he murmured.

'You.'

'I reckon you don't let yourself go often enough. Right?'

'Probably,' she confessed, 'but today has been an unforgettable experience and probably the most fun I've had for years. Even if it wasn't a date,' she teased.

Nick grinned. 'It's getting late. Sadly I do believe it's way past time I get you and *Betsy* home,' he sounded reluctant, 'and I prefer not to ride in the dark.'

For Maggie, the slow reflective ride back to Tingara was filled with warm and wonderful thoughts. As the sun sank lower they just rode slower, Maggie noticed. Was Nick keen to prolong their day a while longer, too, or was it for safety reasons?

The heart-warming day had filled her depleted emotions and only made Maggie think of Nick less as her neighbour and friend and more like — what exactly? A potential boyfriend? She didn't know the answer. Yet. But something deeper had definitely kicked into life today with him. And Maggie had to wonder if that was his intention.

When Nick steered them into her driveway,

Maggie knew she had a six pack of his favourite beer in her refrigerator and she could offer him a drink. But did she dare when he covered her again with that lingering suggestive gaze as they both removed their helmets and he looked at her like she was good enough to eat?

Maggie forced her legs to work and moved away. 'I had a great day. Thanks.'

'Me too.'

Because Maggie had physically and emotionally pulled away, Nick hesitated, making no advances but giving her a dangerous promising stare.

Nick didn't return home as Maggie expected. Instead, she noticed from her front bedroom window moments later that he turned the bike around and headed back into town. She wondered where he was going and why? None of her business of course. Much later as she sat up in bed trying hard to concentrate on bookwork on her laptop after spending a highly charged day with Nick Logan, she thought she heard a motor bike and, from behind the drapes, saw headlights flash onto the cottage. It idled for a long time out the front.

Nick? She caught her breath. Of course she could be mistaken. It could be any other motor bike but Maggie believed she recognised *Betsy's* distinctive engine note after sitting astride her all day. Eventually the noise faded. Until then Maggie hadn't realised she was holding her breath. She felt Milly jump onto the bed and curl up against her legs in her favourite position.

'I hope your paws are clean,' Maggie murmured.

The tiny scamp had an adventurous spirit and explored every corner of the garden. But after her wonderful day with Nick, she didn't really care. She sighed with contentment, turned off the laptop and tried to sleep.

# 8

Less than twelve hours later Nick was at Maggie's back door. The sight of him filled her with a pure rush of pleasure. He was seeking her out again so soon? As she glimpsed his beaming suntanned face through the screen door, her heartbeat stepped up.

'Morning,' he said softly.

'Hey. Coming in?' She held the door open for him. 'Everything all right?' she asked because he suddenly turned serious.

'Will be in a moment.'

He slid a big strong arm about her waist, pulled her against him and kissed her long and deeply. Maggie felt like he'd just given her a dose of some wonderful healing elixir. Her body relaxed. *This* is what she needed? It was a while before either made a move to break apart. Maggie waited to prolong the flooding sensation of being loved and held. It thrilled her that this man had found the courage and need to come bowling next door to satisfy his need this early in the day.

When he finally let her go, Nick murmured, 'Should have done that yesterday. Been thinking about it all night.'

*Me too.* 'Glad you did.'

'Yeah, I got that impression.'

Maggie was fully aware that this moment had just hitched up their relationship to another level. Did she want it? And all it meant? You know what, she thought, to hell with it. She decided to ignore all excuses and reasoning and overthinking. Why not just go with her feelings and let *this* happen? Whatever it turned out to be.

'Have a favour to ask.' Nick leant against the kitchen counter, muscled arms and legs crossed.

She shrugged. 'Fire away.' She would rather have another kiss, feel his warmth and body against her but she waited to hear what he had to say.

'That kiss wasn't by way of influence. It came from need but would you be my plus one to Mal and Emma's wedding?'

Maggie smiled. 'I've been invited too.'

'I know.' He did? He grinned. 'I want to be with you and it makes sense to go together.'

She had the cheeky thought to say *Let's not be too sensible.* 'I'd love to accept. On one condition.' His brows rose. 'That we don't go on *Betsy.*'

He chuckled. 'But you love her.'

'True. But she has her time and place.' And she looked forward to it again one day soon.

He moved forward, brushed her cheek with his hand and pushed it up into her hair, kissing her again until she grew weak. Afterwards he groaned, 'I really need to get to work.'

'Yeah. Damn.'

They both laughed, he stole another slow sexy kiss on her already softly tingling mouth and was gone.

*Welcome to Monday,* Maggie mumbled to

120

herself, smiling, as she tried to concentrate on her day and remember what she was meant to be doing.

She had been slightly nervous about attending Emma's wedding, facing all her family and friends alone. Milly mewed at her feet so Maggie scooped her up.

'I'm a plus one. How about that?' And pretty much hummed as she worked for the rest of the day.

★　★　★

Spring tourism increased. Maggie's first seedlings went out to Ted's hardware and Ivy's shop with new batches coming on all the time. She delighted in the milder pre summer days. Sprinkled with regular warm showers of rain the earth released its new life everywhere, floral colour blazed across Tingara, bee hummed with excitement and breezes sent perfumes into the air.

She worked between the greenhouse and rejuvenating sections of her garden. Digging up one area at a time before planting. Her memorial rose burst into bud. Milly played hide and seek, fruitlessly chasing butterflies and Nick paid regular visits, apologising for his busy trucking schedule at this time of year but seeing Maggie's equal industry.

Often after the boys were in bed, Nick called into Maggie's cottage of an evening to talk, wrapped her into his arms, stole welcome kisses and discussed their days.

Emma and Mal's wedding loomed.

Maggie thrilled to be invited to a hen's night and included among Emma's close friends. The same night, the men were all banished to Will's house. The girls took over Emma's cottage where Maggie met Hannah, a gorgeous blonde with a lovely English accent, now a happily married woman with glittering new rings on her left hand.

Hannah related her journey of romance with Will. Her blue eyes sparkled as she spoke of him but dimmed when she revealed the sad reason — the joint loss of her parents in a road accident for which she felt responsible. The need to face her demons and cross the world in search of personal healing. The peace at St. Anne's renovated chapel a few doors down Gum Tree Lane where she was not only destined to restore her life's balance with Will's help but also find love.

Emma and her friends were no longer carefree teenagers but older now, each touched by experience, grief, divorce or betrayal. Embarking on second chances and new phases in their lives. Maggie secretly prayed hers would become one of them and felt in harmony and welcomed among them.

The only difficulty she faced was seeing and being introduced to Emma's very pregnant sister, Julie, down from Sydney for the event, blossoming and smiling.

That could have been me.

A knot of envy pierced her soul but Julie had also suffered a similar mishap so this child would be doubly precious. Maggie offered a silent prayer all went well for the bride's expectant sister, put a smile on her face and determined to enjoy her growing friendship not only for this evening but the imminent wedding.

Maggie was teased when the girls learned she and Nick were attending as each other's plus one. She played it down, saying each had been invited, they were neighbours and good friends who enjoyed each other's company.

'Nick said it made sense and I agreed.'

A few private side glances and rolled eyes revealed reservations on her excuses but she ignored them.

'Typical serious Nick,' they chuckled, presuming to know him well. And they probably did. On a friendship level. But Maggie smiled to herself knowing she was growing familiar with him in a totally different way.

When Emma and Mal's wedding day finally arrived, Maggie grew as excited as she imagined a bride would be. She and Nick had grown closer in the intervening weeks. She fussed with her appearance, brushed her already glossy thick hair and slipped on the pink lace vintage dress that perfectly draped her figure. Because she wanted to be totally feminine for Nick, she added a double strand of pearls at her throat and glitzy heels.

When Nick came for her, he blew her mind. In a charcoal suit, he looked like a walking god. At first sight, she just wanted to rip off that crisp white shirt and explore the bare skin beneath. Topped by his sleek sandy hair, his waves smoothed into submission, and handsome clean shaven face that split into an irresistible smile, the man to be her escort for the day simply took her breath away.

Nick slowly shook his head and after a low soft whistle in a husky voice he said, 'Maggie Ellis you are one luscious woman.'

'Thank you. My ego is now off the scale.'

'Don't suppose I can kiss off that lipstick?'

'Cheeky.' This man had flipped her heart. She dared not contemplate the future just yet but it sure held promise. 'Haven't you had enough lately.'

'Never,' he growled, leaning forward to capture the lips he pretty much owned lately anyway.

Maggie refreshed her lip gloss and draped the lace shawl about her shoulders. Nick told her the boys were safely with friends for the day and a sleepover that night then offered his arm and they were away.

After two awful traumatic events this past year, Maggie doubted she would ever feel as fulfilled and content with her new life in every way. But she certainly did today. She almost feared it was too good to be true and couldn't possibly last.

When they arrived at Emma and Mal's lovely bluestone cottage, parking was tricky but they eventually found a space. Nick held her hand as they walked around to the rear garden where all proceedings would be held. Maggie noted the gesture of intimacy drew some second glances from the locals and friends that knew them both.

An archway for the ceremony was covered in

greenery and fairy lights with chairs set out under an open sided marquee. Most seats were already full so Nick and Maggie sat toward the back.

Nick leaned closer and whispered a running commentary of family and guests. Pointing out the who's who so she was more familiar with everyone.

'Mal's parents aren't here.'

'Why ever not?'

'They disapproved of his teen relationship and his son Daniel as the result.'

'That could happen to anyone,' Maggie scoffed, 'and it does.'

'They've more or less disowned them.'

Maggie's jaw dropped. 'You're kidding? Even their grandson?' When Nick nodded, she gasped. 'You know what, if you disown family for that reason it's not the child who has failed, it's the parents.'

'It's been tough for him. Meeting Emma has made him happy again. Mal's globetrotting brother, Alex, on the other hand is here though. He works in the Middle East. I believe little Daniel is in the wedding party.'

'Dressed up he'll be so cute.'

Maggie returned Hannah's wave when she turned and caught sight of them. 'Is that her husband Will with long hair?'

'Yep.'

'It's gorgeous.' She sighed. 'Wish mine was as wavy as that.'

'You have beautiful hair.' Nick caught her hand and squeezed it.

Then there was movement behind, Mal and Daniel appeared down the front and the strains of romantic music began to play.

Matron of honour, Julie, wearing a soft pink flowing gown over her tummy so that her pregnancy was barely noticeable, preceded her gorgeous sister bride along the red carpet to the celebrant and her future husband and step son, all standing up the front beneath the arch.

The look Emma and Mal shared when they met touched everyone to tears. The ceremony was simple and heartfelt with the wedding couple exchanging personal vows. Through it all, Maggie occasionally cast a side glance at Nick. He remained absorbed and she wondered if he dwelt on any regrets over his own failed marriage. Perhaps it was far enough in the past that he had let it go.

For herself, although for Maggie it could have been a day of raw confronting emotions on every level because she had always dreamed of this outcome for herself, she saw only a deserving couple committing to their love and with a future life together ahead. So after only the briefest tug of envy, no more than wistful nostalgia, she focused instead on all the positives that such a day held.

A genuine happiness for Emma and Mal, so much in love; a second chance for both in the wake of Emma's divorce and Mal's teen romance that had produced an adorable son and an enforced maturity beyond his years.

The decent man by her side who may become more than a neighbour and friend. Maybe her attraction to Nick was magnified by everything romantic happening around her today. Children running about. Family and friends reunions.

After the ceremony, the chairs were whisked back and tables brought in and set up. Finger food and champagne were handed around, guests mingled. Nick and Maggie joined the line to hug and kiss and shake hands with the newlyweds.

Her new English friend and fellow newcomer to Tingara since becoming Will Bennet's wife, Hannah dragged them away so Maggie could meet her husband. Love was certainly in the air, Maggie mused.

Before they reached him though Hannah whispered, 'So how's it going with Nick then?'

'Oh just fine. We're neighbours so it seemed the logical solution to come together,' she downplayed their situation.

Like everyone else it seemed, Hannah looked sceptical but lovingly introduced her husband as an artist and architect, also explaining his partnership with Mal to develop an eco-subdivision on the edge of town. Maggie was intrigued by the longish wavy hair and cheeky smile. Apparently his cooking skills were renowned and he had just held his first solo art exhibition in the city. A talented man who Hannah clearly adored, revealed in loving glances, touches and private smiles.

'After Emma and Mal come back from their honeymoon, mate, we must all have another one of our social get together meals, okay?' Will said to Nick.

'Sure.'

'Bring Maggie.' He linked Hannah's arm.

'It would be my pleasure.' Nick looked down at her. 'If she's interested.'

'I'd love it.'

Already after only two months in Tingara, Maggie felt so much a part of the community and its people. And, importantly, with Penny so far away now and somewhat alienated in Melbourne, girlfriends.

When Nick excused himself to head off for a chat with mates, Maggie assured him she would be fine. In fact, she had seen Ivy Ashford sitting alone in a corner. Braving a rebuff from the irritable old woman, she headed in her direction.

Choosing comfort over fashion, Ivy normally wore long floral dresses with a baggy cardigan. Today, she looked trim in a grey and white fitted suit with a wide bow flourish at the neck. Something from the Fifties Maggie guessed, possibly hidden in the back of a wardrobe for years. Maybe slightly too big for her now the dear soul was thinner with age. And she still hadn't either managed or bothered to tame her frizzy hair.

'Evening, Ivy.' Maggie sat down uninvited beside her, taking a leaf from Mary's book, ignoring her frostiness and not giving her a chance to argue. 'Mary not around at the moment?' The two old friends had been together all day.

'She's putting Daniel to bed.' Ivy gave her a strange concentrated glance. One of many she had flashed in Maggie's direction all evening and

128

part of the reason she had approached her now.

'That's right. Nick mentioned he's being cared for by his new great granny while Emma and Mal are away. Hannah's looking after her jewellery stall in The Stables for the week.' Ivy didn't respond so she went on, 'It's been a lovely romantic day, hasn't it?'

Boosted by a few glasses of fizz and Nick's warm undivided attention all day, Maggie's confidence ran high and she wondered if a few hints and a dose of Ivy's own forthright honesty wouldn't go astray. It was sad and bothered her that any person would hold onto their bitterness and let an old lost love still rule them. Life was so much more of a treasure than that.

'Pity love doesn't work out for everyone but I intend to keep trying. Despite giving my heart and a decent chunk of my life to a man who didn't want it.'

Ivy squirmed in her seat. 'You with Nick Logan?'

'We're friends. Maybe it's time to move on.'

'He's a good man.'

'We're taking our time.'

Ivy was silent a long while then muttered, 'Don't waste any.'

Maggie concealed her surprise. So, the older woman *did* regret the past? Well, didn't everyone to some extent. Life was full of lessons.

She leant closer to the tiny bird of a woman with her scary hair and dated clothes, nudging her shoulder. 'You speaking from experience?' she teased, knowing her story and shamelessly hoping to draw her out.

'Maybe,' she snapped. 'Life's short. Especially when you're on the tail end of it.'

'I guess we'll all find out one day.' Maggie paused. 'Anything you would do differently?' she quietly probed for a reaction and held her breath.

'Of course.'

So, no explanation then, Maggie sighed, having tried and failed to draw out this lonely resentful woman. 'I'd love children of my own.'

'I never had time.'

So that was her excuse. After being crossed in love, Ivy Ashford had hidden behind work but she was opening up. 'Did you come from a big family?'

'Yep. Ten of us.'

'Wow. I guess you would have plenty of nieces and nephews then. And their children by now?'

Ivy shook her head. 'Don't bother.'

Had she cut herself off from family completely? If so, how tragic. Her story grew ever more cheerless but at least she had shared a little of herself. Daunted by Ivy's sour nature, Maggie guessed few people would push beyond their first impression and bother to ask.

From her years in a florist shop, she had discovered there were hidden stories in everyone's lives. Ivy had probably heard them all too. The reasons and occasions flowers were sent in love, sympathy, thanks and apology.

In future, Maggie determined she would bombard this crusty old soul with friendship. Whether she wanted it or not. Mary was a loyal friend but Maggie doubted there were many others. With her cantankerous attitude, Ivy would have long ago turned them away.

'My seedlings selling?' Maggie thought it best to move onto more neutral ground.

'Could use more.'

Apparently that was a yes. 'Wonderful. I'll bring them in on Monday. Same again?'

Ivy nodded. The sounds of easy listening music with a strong country and western influence had filtered over to them as they chatted and now Nick suddenly emerged from around the perimeter of the dancers taking to the floor.

'That's where you are, Miss Ashford,' he nodded to her in greeting.

'Ivy.'

'I'd like to steal Maggie away to dance if you don't mind.'

'How do you know I can?' she teased.

'If you can't then we'll make a perfect pair and shuffle around the floor together.'

Maggie made to rise but Ivy stayed a thin hand on her arm. 'You look lovely, dear.'

'Thank you. To be honest,' she confided, 'I found this lovely dress in the op shop.'

'I know. It was mine.'

Maggie was staggered. And was that the first smile to threaten Ivy's face she had ever seen?

'It's beautiful. I love it.'

Instinctively, Maggie leant down and hugged her, feeling thin shoulder bones beneath her hands. The woman stiffened and shrank from her impulsive gesture of emotion.

'No good to me anymore,' Ivy snapped.

131

As Maggie held Nick's hand and moved away from Ivy in a daze over what she had just learned, Nick frowned in concern. 'You okay?'

'Stoked.' She beamed. 'Because I'm with you. And I think I've just cracked Ivy's hard shell. This dress — '

'I heard.'

On their way to the dance area, Maggie glimpsed Mary's return and moved across to intercept her. 'You knew about Ivy's dress.' It wasn't a question.

At first Mary looked surprised then confided, 'Forgive me, dear. Ivy's grey now but she had your colouring when she was young. Hard to imagine that the dress fitted her once. She's so skinny now. She had quite the figure but she's shrunk.' Mary sighed. 'She had some exquisite clothes when she was young. Sewing and gardening are her forte. It took her courage to part with them but as she's getting older, she's slowly letting go and passing them on. She's hoarded them in her old wardrobe for over fifty years. Holding on, you know. So treasure this one, my dear.'

'I already do.'

Nick waited patiently then they joined the other couples in the centre of the marquee. His arms circled her waist and Maggie linked hers behind his neck as they began to slow dance in perfect rhythm and harmony.

'You've done this before,' Nick murmured, their faces a breath apart.

'So have you. It's been a beautiful wedding.'

'It's not over yet. Night's still young.'

Heat and wanting curled through Maggie's

body and her heart beat faster with joy and promise. Nick had been protective of her all day with a guiding arm at her elbow or gently at her waist. Making her feel respected and cherished, readily included among his friends.

He moved her in deeper ways she now realised she'd never known. Initial attraction had already sparked and both were guilty of holding back. But it would be a cinch to give in and fall for Nick Logan. If she let herself go. Was Nick up for another long term commitment? How did you know and decide it was real and lasting true love when there were so many variables in life and you were guarded about what the future held?

Nick already had a family. He may not want more. She did. Children of her own. A knot of pain arose in her stomach at the memory of the one she had already lost. Had it been a boy or a girl? Would she ever experience the chance to have more?

Maybe she was getting ahead of herself but the way her emotions and the signals were developing from Nick, it didn't hurt to be realistic and consider the bigger picture.

The need for her own home and family had never faded. She knew this and moving to a small country town meant less population and therefore men. Even if they were available, they would be recycled like her or divorced like Nick, with families already.

Which bumped her attention back to the present to catch the man of her thoughts looking fondly down at her with those dreamy brown eyes and grinning.

'You've been staring across the tent on another planet,' he said.

'Weddings make you reflective.'

'They sure make you wonder. Everything else okay?'

He pressed his cheek against her hair, perhaps so she couldn't see him when she answered. She knew what he meant.

'Good days and bad. Taking one at a time.'

'Good girl.'

Then she let herself feel weak and relaxed in Nick's arms, their bodies aligned full length, mellow from wine and the romantic day and this burning attraction building within.

Knowing without needing any words to express it that Nick felt the same way. He had already told her with deep longing glances from his sexy expressive eyes, from constant touching, thoughtful gestures and making her feel respected and special.

Her heart sang but her head disagreed. With her feelings running so intense and profound, it was so much simpler to just set them free. Because, bottom line, she wanted them to be. See where this budding romance led, so different at this point in her life from the few other attachments she'd ever had.

When the music ended and the dancers drifted away, Nick didn't release her hand but entwined their fingers. Marking his claim? And Maggie wanted it that way. To hell with consequences. It was unproductive and driving her nuts. She wanted Nick in her life because of the undeniable chemistry charged between them

134

but also because he was so supportive, a humble gentleman and an all-round good man who loved his sons. That said a lot about a person right there.

As the evening grew late, guests said their goodbyes and trickled away.

'Ready to go when you are,' Nick said, prompting a decision but leaving it to her. She nodded. They caught up with Hannah and Will, saying farewells and all promising to catch up soon.

Emma and Mal's happiness glowed from them both as Nick and Maggie thanked them for the invitations to share their memorable day. The women hugged, the men shook hands and goodnights were called out as they left.

Maggie could feel Nick's mischievous mood hum as they walked in the crisp starry night out to his shiny white ute. Its throaty engine note roared into life on the still air. She pulled her shawl about her shoulders for the short drive through the sleepy main street and out to Stony Creek Way. Home.

As they pulled into her driveway and Nick cut the engine, he didn't mince words. 'Not too keen on ending the night just yet so I hope you're planning to offer me a nightcap.'

'I am now,' she laughed.

That was a proposition if ever she heard one. Where would the night lead?

# 9

Nick leapt from behind the wheel and was around to Maggie's side of the vehicle opening the door before she could change her mind.

He helped her out, stole a seductive kiss in the dark and held her hand all the way to the back door. Inside, his hand stalled hers before she turned on a light.

'Dark is good.'

Maggie hadn't felt this turned on by a man in years and the promise of what they could be together. Nick took control and cupped her backside with his big hands, pressing her erotically against him. Full length. Everything he did exploded her senses and longing. Each time he caressed her, running his hands all over her as far as he could reach, blood pulsed through her yielding body. She couldn't get enough of this man and his loving. His long slow kisses left her weak.

Maggie lost track of time but eventually, breathing heavily, she grew aware of Nick growling, 'I'd explore more but as much as my body craves you, I don't want to ruin that beautiful dress.'

Maggie sighed. 'Nick — '

He stopped her with a gentle finger against her lips. 'I know you've suffered a recent ordeal and you're still coping with the fallout. Just need you to know how I feel about you.'

'I get the message,' she whispered.

He pushed his hands up into her hair and drove her wild again with another long sexy kiss of exploration and excitement she never wanted to end. When it did, he kept nibbling her lips and ears and the dip in her neck, possibly the most erotic and vulnerable place on her entire body.

'For some reason,' she gasped as he continued his magic, 'I need to sit down. Snap on that switch behind me.' She could see he was about to object so she added quickly, 'Just for a moment. I'll be right back.'

When light flooded the cottage, they both frowned against the sudden glare. Maggie kicked off her heels and disappeared, returning moments later with an armful of fat candles and setting them all out on the low sitting room table.

'Here, light these.' She handed him a taper.

'What is it with women and candles?'

She flickered her eyebrows. 'They're romantic.'

'Ah. Best light them then, I guess.'

Maggie went to the decanter on her small sideboard and poured a generous splash of French cognac into her best glasses before adding ice and settling against Nick on the sofa.

He spread his arm around her shoulder, drawing her close. 'To . . . life?'

'Absolutely.'

Maggie was relieved when he didn't say *us* but he understood the unknowns between them both. At some point, the time would come for them to discuss deeper issues but for now, tonight was enough for both. They sipped their drinks and enjoyed the intimacy of candlelight, silence, indulging in kisses they couldn't resist and a comfortable familiarity.

'You've bowled me over, Maggie, since you came,' Nick drawled. 'You're an unbelievably gorgeous woman who I can't believe is showing any interest in an old divorced father like me. You make my days lighter. I feel less like a Dad and more like a real man again. Younger. Knowing you has given me hope for the future. Without the right woman, I didn't realise how lonely I'd been.'

That any man should speak of her in such glowing terms as a woman and the impact she had on his life was humbling.

'You've been there for me, too, since the day I arrived. Helping me put up the greenhouse, including me among your friends. You're a kind hearted lovely man. Nick Logan. Never underestimate your worth. You are no *old father* but one rather sexy man who I count not only as a neighbour and friend but much more now. And you were there for me when I needed someone most.'

She turned away, choking up, and he squeezed her hand. She was finding it a slow process to reclaiming true happiness but Nick filled her with hope and warmth and trust.

'I'm falling for you, Maggie.' He gazed deep into her eyes, his meaning clear. 'I'd like to be around for you for a long time to come.'

He was on the prowl for her and she knew it. Even thrilled at the thought of the chase to come when she planned to be caught. 'Maybe not tonight. I can't do this yet.'

'Sure.' He raised her hand and kissed it. 'I'm right next door.'

But when Nick kissed her hungrily again, it was so easy to forget every other warning instinct. Like what she was getting into here. If she and Nick continued as they were, growing closer and feeling deeper, she already knew. Yes, it would be a responsibility to help raise his sons but would he still want her and welcome her into his family on terms of her own?

★ ★ ★

Maggie was in euphoric heaven over Nick's declaration on Saturday night after the wedding. With reservations because of the mental barrier created by her long held dream that the years had failed to fade. For her own crazy reason.

So with her hands up to the wrists in dirt potting up in the greenhouse, she barely registered when her mobile rang. She recognised Penny's number, frowned and answered the call.

'Hi. This is a lovely surprise,' Maggie said. It had been months.

'I know. My bad. How is everything up there?'

She was fishing. Something about this call didn't feel quite right. Feeling guilty for doing so, Maggie immediately grew suspicious. With Pen's tendency to spread news, stakes were high she had called to rave over something.

With every passing week and feeling so settled in Tingara, Maggie began to care less and less about her previous city life and wondered what prompted Penny's sudden contact. Good news or bad, her friend thrived on both. Even before leaving Melbourne, Maggie was tiring of Penny's shallow grapevine babble.

She briefly covered her recent doings.

'Wow, I'm surprised you know anyone well enough already to be invited to a wedding.'

I'm not, Maggie thought, detecting a note of jealousy in Penny's voice, because I live in a small town now and know the inclusive Tingara community.

'Not really. The locals are so welcoming and friendly it doesn't take much time to feel at home.'

She had no intention of telling Penny that she didn't attend alone. Her friend would assume she had.

'Looks like I'll have to come visit and see for myself.'

Penny leave Melbourne? Amazing. Maggie suddenly twigged that had been her intention all along. Strange to be feeling so wary of an old friend and how distance helped you see them more clearly.

'You have a standing invitation any time.'

In a flash, Penny replied, 'How about next weekend?'

Four days. Before his wedding, Mal had finished knocking out the old kitchen and installing the new one so she would be proud to show off her finished country cottage to her friend. She could finish painting indoors this week. The old curtains and blinds had already been replaced with ready-mades from Ted's hardware store. That shop sold everything.

'Wonderful. I trust the GPS will get you here and you won't get lost in the bush,' Maggie teased.

'I'm looking forward to it.' There was a pause. 'I have news.'

Of course she did. Maggie's heart lurched that it was something she couldn't tell her over the phone but covered her concern with a light hearted, 'I figured.'

By Friday night, the cottage was scrubbed and gleaming, a casserole simmered atop the Aga and Penny's favourite chocolate walnut cake was baking in the oven. The spare room was freshened up with new linen and a posy of fragrant spring flowers from Ivy's shop. The only dampener was the reason for Penny's visit. Not unlikely it involved Leon. What was the latest?

With summer time now in place, Penny had decided to drive up tonight, leaving work early, making use of the extra evening daylight. So Maggie's first house guest was arriving soon. She still held mixed feelings about her stay but genuinely looked forward to it, if not the purpose.

It had only been months but Maggie felt sentimental at first sight of Penny again, her familiar face the embodiment of her old life in the city. Which was both good and bad for it also brought up memories of other things. Ironically as they hugged in greeting, Maggie knew it also meant listening to endless tales. She could endure it for a weekend.

Penny had made the effort but Maggie frowned as to why. So unlike her friend not to blurt it right out. Too awful to disclose over the phone? She shivered against such negative thoughts. She must tread carefully this weekend about any mention of Nick in her life. Her growing romance was too new and special to be broadcast and possibly distorted. So she felt rotten for not being able to confide.

'Oh this is cute,' Penny said exploring the cottage later, exclaiming with delight over her lovely room for the weekend.

Over dinner, her friend observed, 'You seem happy. Country life is obviously meant for you.'

'Must be all the fresh air and physical work I'm doing every day.' Maggie passed off Penny's watchful gaze of assessment. 'I'll show you my greenhouse in the morning. I'm so proud of it.' She almost added *Nick helped me build it* but stopped herself just in time.

Following dinner over which they caught up on each other's lives, Penny was distracted and clearly had something else on her mind. Maggie's heart sank. So when they curled up on the sitting room sofa and Milly leapt up onto her lap, she found stroking the kitten helped ease her growing tension. She couldn't wait to raise the issue on Penny's mind. It had to be about Leon. If so, she needed to know and get it over with, annoyed with herself for even showing interest.

'You said you had news.'

Penny squirmed and Maggie prepared herself. 'I suppose you might guess it's about Leon. And Natalia.'

'I'm not really interested,' she lied, 'but you've come all this way.'

'Living up here you won't have heard.'

'What now?' Maggie sipped her mug of tea, faking disinterest, tempted to eat another slice of cake out of frustration. 'Don't tell me they're getting married.' *Or I'll bleed.*

'Well, actually, yes.'

Maggie flinched. She had waited Ten Whole Years for a proposal and this *girl* was asked within months?

'It's worse,' Penny added.

'Can't be.'

'Afraid so.'

'Spit it out, then, I'm a big girl now. I've moved on.' But had she? Her heart still ached in distress at the thought of what might have been and in advance of what she suspected was to come.

'Are you quite sure you want to hear this?' Penny insisted.

'Oh for heaven's sake, Penny, you've come all this way,' Maggie snapped, gripped by exasperation and a cold wave of dread.

'They're having a baby.'

Stunned, Maggie stared into space while her whole world stopped. 'The bastard,' she hissed.

Penny sidled closer. 'You okay?'

'What do you think?' Maggie flashed. 'No I'm bloody well not!'

Milly mewed in fright and leapt from her lap to the floor, skittering away. The action jolted Maggie back to reality. She had forgotten the kitten was even there.

She stood up, fumed and paced. 'I tell you what, tea doesn't cut it. I need alcohol.' She could now, right? Because there was no baby, no feeling, nothing. 'Join me?' Maggie glared at Penny who nodded. 'Wine, or we can go straight to the hard stuff. I have some excellent French cognac.' Which she had drunk with Mr. Wonderful on a far happier evening last weekend.

'All right. Let's go with that,' Penny was barely enthusiastic.

'I'm just being polite. Happy to drink alone,' Maggie said dryly.

'I'm sorry Mags to bring you disappointing news.'

'Disappointing! It's damned criminal.' Maggie was barely able to concentrate and slopped brandy onto the sideboard from careless pouring. 'Blast. Waste of perfectly fine alcohol,' she muttered, licking her fingers and striding to the kitchen for a cloth to mop it up.

'I considered telling you over the phone-'

'Maybe you should have because I may not be much company for a while.' Maggie handed Penny her drink but remained standing.

Penny sipped and coughed. 'Powerful stuff.'

'As long as it works.' Maggie shook her head, her thoughts racing. 'You know what? I feel so used and exploited. Like I was kept dangling until something better came along. Like the fertile body of a sexy Italian goddess. And you know something else?' She squinted at her friend. 'Whenever I spoke about marriage or children, he always fobbed me off.'

Maggie could not say his name she was so furious with rage at his betrayal and sick to think she had allowed herself to be fooled. Blinded and hopeful by what she wanted but had never been his intention to give.

'He never actually said *yes*. Always excuses and reasons to delay a family before which I always hoped there would be a wedding.' She barked out a short laugh. 'But he never actually promised that either. Our entire relationship was based on unspoken promises. Yes, I'm mad at him but how do you think I feel to have been so easily misled and then abandoned?'

Maggie knocked back the last of her drink and dropped back onto the sofa beside Penny, uselessly nursing her empty glass.

'Over the years I buried my despair. Backed off, waited and settled for second best. So I really only have myself to blame for not having the courage to face the reality of our situation and leave.'

'You were great together. In the beginning.'

'Yeah, we were.' She sighed and looked directly at Penny. 'Tell me, how far along is Natalia do you know? I mean, do they have to marry? Did she trap him?' Maggie brightened. 'Now that would be a hoot, huh?'

'Does it really matter? It's done. I wanted you to know, that's all. It was really difficult for me to make the decision to tell you or not. Would you rather have stayed ignorant?'

Maggie shrugged. 'I might have heard from someone else but that's unlikely living in the country now. Perhaps knowing and getting a little drunk will help drum it all out of my system.' She rested a hand on Penny's. 'Sorry to be so foul. I appreciate you coming to tell me. I know you meant well. It's lovely to be together again but in future-'

'I get it.' Penny nodded. 'No more. You should come visit me in the city.'

'And all your cats.' Maggie grinned. 'I'm making a new life and friends. I have everything I need here.'

'Thank you very much.' Penny pretended to be offended.

'Except you, naturally.'

'Don't forget where I live.'

After that, Maggie tried to recapture her initial happier mood of reunion and the anticipation of a girls' catch up weekend but every conversation and smile or laughter felt forced. Both pretended all was well but their time together was spoilt by Penny's revelation.

Her friend grew fidgety and preoccupied, her brain completely out to lunch. She also seemed amused but unimpressed by the small independent shops, leaving Maggie to wonder if Penny had ever been beyond the city limits. Maggie dragged her to The Stables where she introduced Hannah, in charge of Emma's jewellery stall while the newlyweds were on their honeymoon, but the meeting fell flat and they didn't stay long.

As they were leaving and Penny moved on ahead, Hannah must have sensed something amiss. 'You okay?'

'Sure. Probably too much wine and talk,'

146

Maggie said, not to mention lack of sleep.

Even a jaunt into Maggie's beloved country-side didn't enthuse her guest so she cut their tour short and headed back into town. While she cooked dinner, Penny played with Milly but they both struggled to chat over the meal and her friend yawned soon after, claiming a busy day and headed for bed. Later, Maggie noticed the light still on under the door in the guest room. What had happened to their friendship that Penny preferred reading to Maggie's company? Fair enough, she wasn't the brightest sparkler at the moment but surely Pen understood that?

Sunday morning Penny slept late. No wonder. She had stayed up reading half the night. She exclaimed over Maggie's cooked breakfast of bacon and eggs, and pancakes but declared with the long drive ahead back to Melbourne she would prefer to leave before lunch.

Deflated, Maggie didn't even bother to mention her pride and joy greenhouse for Penny neither asked nor showed any interest in anything connected with her friend's new country life.

She should have just phoned. It would have saved them both time and embarrassment. Besides, Maggie begrudged what she considered a wasted weekend when she could have been with Nick who had been totally understanding when she explained about her friend's visit and their girls' weekend. But now, after Penny's bombshell, she needed time alone to process her last lingering feelings of hurt and regret.

So it was with mixed emotions that Maggie

waved her friend goodbye, both grateful it seemed for the reprieve. How could a lifetime friendship sink to this? Distance? Had they only stayed friends from habit? Not had all that much in common all along?

As Penny drove off down Stony Creek Way into town on her way back to Melbourne, Maggie's shoulders dropped in relaxation and she set her feelings free.

Uneasy and confused, she didn't feel like returning indoors nor even getting back to the work she loved in the greenhouse. It was Sunday, the weekend, for heaven's sake. She would take some time to herself. So she set off striding with no purpose or destination in mind, just needing the peace of the surrounding bush and fresh air. From the creek at the bottom of the garden there was a walking track of sorts and she blindly followed it.

Her footsteps pounded the lush spring grass underfoot, her hands clenched and before she had gone more than a few hundred feet, her empty despair cracked. Muttering against the unfairness of what Penny had told her about Leon this weekend and having squandered ten years of her life, tears rolled down her cheeks. Maggie sniffed and wiped them away and kept walking and kept pouring out a steady stream of verbal resentment. Much of it highly coloured.

Emotions she had dammed up since Friday night, an inner tension she had felt obliged to bury during Penny's stay, finally erupted into exasperation together with a renewal of past hurt. Maggie thought she had dealt with all these

148

feelings, moved on. That Leon was wiped from her system but Penny's bombshell opened a small fissure of bitterness.

Magpies and parrots screeched and fluttered off in fright from trees at the sound of her loud raging voice ringing through the bush.

Unaware of time, Maggie had no idea how long it was since she left home and trudged in fury, one foot after the other, along the partly overgrown path, before she sensed someone approaching from her left. She focused long enough to make sure it wasn't some neighbour's charging animal that might have escaped. Instead, she pulled up in shock to see Nick striding down the length of his block and realising this section of the creek ran along the bottom of his property too, but a long way from the house that she could see at a distance behind him.

Still upset with heartache, Maggie couldn't have cared less about her appearance and stared at his approach. He was scowling as though angry.

He stopped right in front of her. 'Maggie? You okay?'

She took a deep breath and swallowed. 'No.'

# 10

Maggie wished she'd had enough presence of mind to bring a bottle of wine but after drowning her self-pity all weekend, her supply was gone. She noticed the path disappeared so there really seemed no point in continuing anyway.

'Anything I can do? Can I help?' Nick asked.

She shook her head, not at all embarrassed that her neighbour should see her in such a state. After all, he had seen her in a far worse situation. Maggie turned toward the cool dark rushing waters of Stony Creek and the leafy carpet underfoot. She heard Nick's footsteps follow.

He pulled up beside her. 'Saw Penny leave. You two had a row?'

Maggie barked out a short laugh. 'No. She just brought bad news. Can my life get any more pathetic and hopeless?' she muttered as she lowered her exhausted self to sit on the ground in the dappled shade of a river gum. She picked up a dry leaf and played with it.

Nick didn't ask if he could stay and join her, just hunkered down alongside, hanging his arms over his bent knees.

'Wanna talk?' he murmured, probing.

Maggie slowly shook her head in warning. 'I'm gonna talk dirty and rough.'

'Nothing a truckie hasn't heard before I'll bet.'

'How come you're such a gentleman, then?'

'Choice.'

'Fair enough.' Maggie paused before the mere direction of her thoughts filled her with anger again. 'My ex-partner Leon is a bloody lying bastard swine — '

'Don't hold back.'

'-who wouldn't marry me and kept putting off having a family but within months of dumping me is now engaged and has knocked up his new sexy siren child bride-to-be.'

Nick whistled low. 'Damn.' The silence of the bush and their stalled conversation fell around them. 'You're not exaggerating. He does sound like . . . what you said.'

'I gave that man the best years of my life while I waited for his proposal and telling me I could quit taking the pill. My mistake.'

'Best years of your life are still ahead I'd say. You're only, what, around thirty?'

Maggie chuckled in surprise. 'Thanks. You're easily fooled and fabulous for the ego.'

Nick chuckled, deep and throaty, in the way that always made Maggie melt. That sound was so sexy. 'You're hardly over the hill. Pretty hot actually.'

She squirmed with embarrassment. Looking a mess like she did, feeling exposed. 'You need glasses,' she muttered.

After a moment, he said, 'I find it hard to imagine why any man would replace you in his life,' then paused and asked, 'What's she like?'

Maggie smirked, trying not to feel jealous, be generous, stay a lady. Then remembered she had already shot that image to pieces in front of this

151

man she liked and respected so much.

'Let's just say the few times I've ever seen her, those implanted boobs are never completely inside any outfit she wears. Either Leon lied to me for years or his little tramp is either stupid or careless or very very smart. Whatever, he deserves her. I hope they're utterly miserable together. She's a party girl. High maintenance,' Maggie explained. 'She won't want her figure spoilt so she'll eat lettuce for nine months, and breast feeding? Don't even go there. I bet this wasn't planned. A huge mistake. God I hope so,' she growled.

Nick edged closer and pressed his leg and shoulder against hers. 'Does it matter what they do or why?' he asked quietly.

His comment made Maggie pause in thought. She turned and stared at him, not liking it but realising he was right. She was wasting energy staying angry. Somehow she had to move past this crushing news and let it go. But surely she was allowed to grieve and vent a little first? What did that achieve? She was done. Leon and his sexpot could rot. Deepest hurt was knowing that probably neither of them would really embrace being parents. But who knew? Stranger things had happened.

'I've already told Penny I don't want to hear anything anymore.'

'As your friend she probably means well but it can't be helping. Don't let a sour relationship define your life.'

Maggie pulled a wry grin. 'I thought I was okay but this latest news has rocked me. Took a lot of pain to finally realise it but he was never for me.'

'Well if he was, he'd have to stand in line.'

Maggie slowly turned to look at him. Nick wasn't joking. He was serious. His warm steady gaze told her so. Agonising over one man now pushed into her past and thrilled by the intimate words of love from another. All in the same moment.

'That's some confession,' she said softly.

'Mean it.'

'I can see that. I'm . . . flattered.'

Nick shrugged. 'I'm trained in self-defence anyway. He'd lose.'

'Top thought.'

'Look ahead not back. Don't stay in the past.'

'Do you?'

'Yeah mostly. Forget sometimes but only for the boys. Their mother will never know how much she gave up by walking out of their lives.'

'You have three beautiful sons. I barely know them but I already feel . . . attached,' she admitted.

'Noah has taken to you especially. He was only three when his mother left. Even seeing her occasionally, he's not seemed to form a bond. Yet. But she's not in his life all that much. Maybe when he's bigger.'

'That's sad. For him. You're so blessed to have those boys. I'd give anything for children of my own. And don't say it will happen,' she added quickly, 'there's no guarantee.'

The whole Leon issue weighed heavily on her mind, raised afresh since Penny's disclosure.

153

Talking to Nick always seemed to help. It felt so right being around him but above all she knew she could rely on him, trust him and her confidences were safe.

'Knowing what's come to light now,' Maggie continued, 'Leon just didn't want children with me. He should have at least been honest with me.' She frowned. 'Maybe I pushed too much. If I'm honest, I've always been on about it. After we split and I sat down and thought about it, I decided on taking matters into my own hands, as you know. Turns out it didn't even work out being a single mum either.'

The last words caught in her throat. Nick finally sat down beside her on the grass and took her hand for a squeeze, entwining their fingers. She loved the touch of him. Just having him near. He had become her anchor.

'Sounds like being a mother is really important to you. Can I ask why?'

Maggie stiffened. 'No one has ever asked me that before.'

'Because they didn't ask?' Maggie nodded. 'So what's your answer?'

God this man was digging deep. Her fearful voice lowered to barely above a whisper. 'It's kind of . . . illogical and I've never shared my dream with anyone. Always knew people would think me crazy.'

She hesitated, stalling for time and looked down toward the creek slowly sliding by.

'I'm a surviving twin. My sister, Susanna, was stillborn.' Maggie smiled to herself as she felt Nick shift beside her. 'I've always thought my

154

name, Margaret, was so old fashioned. I mean, what were my parents thinking in the seventies? But I loved Susanna. Even from a young age I grew up knowing about her. My parents told me and I understood. It's not really guilt of surviving that I feel. It's more a need to nurture. I've always hated seeing things die. Being introduced into gardening by my spinster aunts gave me such hope and positive joy. I loved to watch seeds pop up from the soil into tiny green shoots and become plants that thrived and flowered or bore fruit.'

Here, Maggie paused to catch her breath in apprehension over Nick's reaction.

'So as far back as I can remember I've always felt this deep longing to have a child and call her Susan to replace my sister.'

'Ah.' Nick was silent a moment. 'It's a beautiful tribute but what if you had a son?'

Maggie smiled through damp eyes. 'Always a possibility. Everyone knows you can't replace another human being,' she said honestly. 'I planted a white scented rose called *Susan* in my garden in memory of my little lost soul recently. It's actually given me peace. A part of me was able to let go after I did that one small thing. Now every time I walk by in the garden I see the bush coming into leaf and bud and I know that little angel will always be with me.'

Nick spread an arm around her shoulder, drawing her close. Pressed a kiss into her hair then nuzzled her ear and cheek. Maggie's reflections were shot. A magical thing in every way. She closed her eyes, hearing only Nick's breath so close, feeling a soft breeze play with her hair and her body unwind every nerve end, allowing his attentions to rule.

It seemed the most natural thing in the world every time he kissed her and this morning was no different. His warm seeking mouth claimed hers with such touching softness their lips melted together as though it was meant to be.

'No pressure, and I know you're still dealing with lots of stuff,' he murmured, 'but I need more of you, Maggie Ellis. Lots more.'

He nibbled her ear, shooting wonderful sensations up and down her body. She sighed with desire and contentment as he kissed the dip of her neck and she leant her head to snuggle against him.

'You're taking my mind off *everything*. In the best way.'

'Haven't lost my touch then?'

'Not from where I'm sitting.'

He plunged a hand into her hair, kissed her again and they sank back onto the grass. Drowning beneath his touch and the stirring need building inside whenever she was with him, Maggie's mind blanked to all but Nick's wandering hands. For the first time she allowed him to freely explore over the body she had always disliked. Over her curves, and she sure had plenty of those. Beneath her shirt.

His hair was thick and soft through her fingers, his mouth possessive and stirring.

She stopped suddenly and whispered, 'Where are the boys?'

Nick groaned at being forced back to reality.

'With mates. What a passion killer!' He rolled away onto his back, thrusting a hand across his face.

'Sorry.'

Maggie rolled over to drape herself across his chest and take the lead, giving back something of what she had just taken away. Her hands discovered every masculine line of his face. When her finger slowly traced the outline of his mouth, he playfully nipped it.

'Falling for you, Maggie.'

To be honest, he had flipped her heart, too. Nick naked filled her mind with fantasies to imagine what their bodies could do together, erotic thoughts, Maggie growing hot and bothered in the process. But these deeper feelings between them were serious now and deserved consideration. The dynamics of combining two families, their lives, her business, the boys. What now? Where did this take them? Maggie sat up and hugged her knees.

Nick half rose beside her, resting on an elbow. 'Maggie?'

She looked down at him. No denying she loved him. It was fact. 'I feel the same about you. We should talk.'

He chuckled. 'Talking wasn't on my mind.'

'At this hour of the day? In broad daylight?'

Maggie pretended to be scandalised, all previous gloomy thoughts of her past banished from her mind. But her heart beat just a bit faster at the racy thought. Handy that Nick's radar had sought her out. He always seemed to be around when she needed him. But if they intended taking their feelings forward, certain important issues, at least for her, needed consideration. She hesitated to plunge ahead and give herself to this rather adorable warm hearted loving man before dealing with the matters on her mind.

Nick pushed himself up and extended his arms to help Maggie up.

He wrapped his arms around her waist. 'You need more time.'

Her hands spread over the soft cotton of his blue checked shirt. 'A bit.'

'Anything in particular on your mind?'

Maggie shrugged, afraid to voice it and pulled away to turn and stare down to the creek again. She sensed Nick standing right behind her.

'You want to continue going along as we are?' she heard him say.

'What are we?'

'Neighbours who became friends and are now much more. You know I'm thinking long term with you, Maggie. Making you a part of my life.'

His tone softened and she ached to turn into his arms but needed space.

'We have something powerful and physical that's hit us both.' He put his hands on her shoulders, turning her to face him before stepping back and sinking his hands into his pockets. 'Why don't we focus on some positives? I'll go first.'

He cleared his throat and Maggie knew it was time to be brave and honest.

'Since Rachel left, I believed I could be father *and* mother to my sons. Male pride thing, too, feeling inadequate, a failure.'

'You're not a failure,' she scoffed, recalling him having voiced that concern before. 'You didn't walk away. I can see it's a tough job raising a family alone.'

'So I'm discovering. The boys like having you around. I can tell. Tyler would never say but I can tell Chris and Noah do. I watch them with you and I watch you with them. They like you.'

'I hope so.'

'I thought neither I nor the boys needed another woman in our lives and home. Until I met you.' He paused. 'When you smile at me like that I'm lost. Since you've come to town my load feels lighter. You're one warm sensitive lady, so sexy, but totally unaware you have that effect on a man. Hell you're even feminine when you're up to your elbows in dirt.'

She laughed, moved by his loving words and feeling unworthy but damn glad he expressed them, finding it difficult to stop herself from reaching out to touch him.

'You love kids and animals, you're a homemaker but also with great ambition and drive in business energy. Doing what you love. You've slid into our family like you've always been there. You've never made me feel less than a man. From early on you offered to help and you hardly knew us. Only a person with an unselfish heart does that. I've pushed through hard times alone but I want and need you in my life. I was smitten with you at first sight.'

He pushed a hand across his face. 'But I realise you've been burned, too, and more recently than me. Second time around's a big step for anybody. And I understand you're still cautious. We've each given our love fully to another person and been let down. You have my word I'll never do that to you,' he promised.

Maggie nodded, unable to speak in the face of such honest and raw admission from Nick.

'I appreciate you might need a while longer to let our relationship grow. I respect that.' He grinned. 'But don't make me wait too long or I'll come and get you.'

Maggie laughed, blown away by the love from Nick that was being freely offered here. What could be more natural and romantic than standing beneath gum trees with Stony Creek gurgling along behind them, its clear waters glinting in the late morning spring sunshine, and having a man confide and share his deepest love for you?

Nick Logan was a solid family man, trustworthy, and she adored him. He drew her like bees were attracted to nectar on flowers. But he was a package deal.

'What are you thinking behind that frown?' Nick asked, sounding unsure.

She hated doing this but it had to be said. 'I'm falling in love with you, Nick. My wildest dreams never imagined another man in my life again that I would feel about like this. You take my breath away for every wonderful reason but especially because you want *me*. And I found you in little old Tingara, right next door,' she grinned. 'How cool is that? You're a devoted and loving human being, a hardworking genuine honest man. A wonderful father, I cherish your boys. Everyone else's children are the family I've never had myself. But — '

This was going to sound so selfish. 'I keep asking myself if I would be content to help raise someone else's children instead of my own flesh and blood. If that would be enough.'

Nick's brows flinched. But he had to know her truth. 'I still ache to have a baby and be a mother myself. You have three sons already. You might be done. Not want any more, and that's a decision I would never ask of you unless you were fully willing.'

'The ideal family doesn't exist,' Nick responded, thoughtful and frowning. 'Speaking as a father, I've tried to do my best under every circumstance. Even if I didn't achieve it, at least I know I aimed for it. My boys deserve nothing less. You work at creating a family, whatever form it takes, for whatever reason. Families will always be different combinations depending on the circumstances and people in then. Yeah, I come with kids and, yeah, you want more. But this is about *us*, Maggie. You and me. Just us,' Nick pointed out. 'It kind of bothers me to think you would only consider loving and marrying me for the babies I can give you.'

Maggie was stunned. Marriage! She knew it was on the horizon, a possibility for the future, but it was on the table already?

'You've already proved you don't need a lover or partner for that.'

Nick's strong statement made Maggie stop and think. Is that what she was doing? Only wanting a man in her life to give her children? Why she and Leon had failed? The ugly possibility also reared its head that this man she faced now could be lost to her, vanish from her life. Right now she would forsake anything not to have that happen. But it might if she persisted with the same mindset.

She braved a gaze into Nick's brown eyes, filled with both steel and compassion. What he suggested challenged Maggie's ingrained approach. Was it time to stop this unaccountable grieving that burned inside for her sister, Susan, and move on?

As a result of Nick's prompting, it was like he had shone a light on her life and for the first time ever, she finally imagined how others might see or misread her obsession. Why hadn't she seen it herself before this?

Nick brushed his thumb tenderly across her trembling mouth.

'I haven't let Susanna go, have I?' she whispered, appalled at the realisation.

'That's a question only you can answer. I get the impression you're putting pressure on yourself. As sincere as your reasons are for feeling that way, you've fixed on this so long in your mind it's become an obligation. So,' Nick speculated cautiously, 'maybe you should consider children if only you yourself dearly want them.'

Maggie stared at him for a long time taking in what he had just suggested. 'My mother was quite open and realistic about Susanna but maybe that's because she always spoke of her as if she was still a part of our lives. Understandable because

162

she was her daughter. Why do *I* feel like this, though, when I was just her sister?'

'Twin sister,' Nick specified. 'I've heard there's a mysterious bond between them.'

'To this extent?'

'Not impossible. You've lived with this all your life so far. Sounds like it's been a difficult approach to break.'

'I didn't even know I needed to.'

Nick gathered her into his strong muscled arms and just held her. 'You have lots to think about. I'll give you some space. Come over when you're ready.' He pulled away. 'You okay?'

'Yes, I believe I am. At least, I will be.'

His face tugged into a slow smile. 'Best be off to get those boys of mine.'

As he turned to head back up the paddock, Maggie said, 'Nick?' He paused and glanced back at her. 'Thanks.'

'Don't stay away too long.'

If he kept flashing that devilish dynamic smile? Unlikely. She watched him stride away, arms swinging, his powerful legs easily eating up the distance ahead of him to the house.

★   ★   ★

Back home, although it was barely midday, Maggie poured a brandy, added a single ice cube — she didn't care to dilute the effect too much — and settled on the sofa with only lamplight and Milly for company.

In her childhood, she wished another daughter for her mother to replace her twin, Susanna.

163

Then before Paul was born, Maggie prayed for a girl but, of course, it was not meant to be. After that, by the time she finished school and studied horticulture, the dream for another sister, Susanna, had somehow turned into a personal desire of her own.

She analysed when it started. From it always being a known part of their family but, over the childhood years, as she grew older so much emphasis was placed on Maggie being a twin, as a result she had gradually assumed an impression of being less important. Because she had always sensed the other half of her was missing.

And birthdays, which in most family circumstances, were special became bittersweet. As though Maggie was never enough. Incredible to think that such a bond of connection could be a psychic and not a physical thing even though Maggie had been the surviving baby and neither knew nor ever saw her sister.

Nick's perception far beyond her own was the catalyst to consider her longing for another Susanna that needed addressing and had the potential to cause future harm in a relationship. He had been upfront and honest enough to confront her with it now, before any chance of damage to their bursting love.

She now realised it was neither her duty nor necessary to replace her sister. Susan had lived if only for the briefest time in her mother's womb, and Maggie must now come to terms with the fact that must be enough.

The space Nick had suggested proved

cleansing. Her mind slowly cleared and she felt fresher with more energy. Not burdened so much by the self-imposed demands of her childhood and recent past.

In the following days, with conviction and determination she was able to walk past her *Susan* rose bush and smile with fondness and not regret or any sense of unfinished business.

# 11

Maggie knew Nick didn't usually drive on weekends but the following Saturday a big urgent job came up so he was away all day on a long haul and not expected back until late.

Before he left, he approached her and she reassured him when he asked whether she would be around in case Zoe disappeared again. He had offered the girl good money for the full day and made her promise he could rely on her this time, but he needed backup in place in case she defaulted.

Maggie said she would be in the greenhouse all day, pop over to the homestead and check on them all now and again, then take over and release Zoe before dark when Maggie would stay for the evening and make dinner for the boys. They always nagged for takeaways but she loved to cook so they had all compromised and decided on her homemade pizzas.

Even as she boxed up her latest seedling orders ready for Monday deliveries and began seeding and planting up more, her yeast dough was rising in the cottage kitchen. Awesome toppings were ready in the fridge and she was due to take it all next door by dusk.

So Maggie was surprised when Tyler appeared at her greenhouse door in the early afternoon, skidding his bicycle to a stop, looking flushed and anxious.

'Hey,' she said, immediately stopping what she was doing and wiped her hands clean. Maggie's body moved to high alert. 'Everything okay?'

'Not really.'

'Zoe still over there?'

'Yeah but I should get back to my brothers. I think we have a problem.'

Maggie rather liked the way he included her in his concern.

'She's got company. Her boyfriend Jake just arrived. Dad doesn't like or trust him and he's just offered me a deal.'

Maggie folded her arms, listening, wondering what on earth was about to come to light and afraid to ask so she allowed Tyler to explain.

'Go on,' she urged gently.

'Jake offered me $100 to deliver a parcel to a bloke in town. Seems a lot of money just for doing that. I would have done it for a couple bucks, you know?' he grinned, 'but that amount's off the scale, right?' Maggie nodded. 'I asked him why he didn't do it himself and he just sneered and said he was *busy*. He was hanging all over Zoe on the sofa. She didn't seem all that comfortable. She tried getting rid of him. Told him to leave but he's staying. I don't want him causing trouble in our house or Zoe to be doing anything against her will, you know?'

Maggie knew exactly what he meant and nodded.

'Besides,' Tyler frowned, 'the stuff looked and smelled funny.'

With her gardening education, Maggie's mind swiftly turned over. 'So, this package, is it like dried leaves, flowers and stems? Shredded or crumbled?'

Tyler nodded madly. 'Smelled kinda off. Looked like loose tobacco like old men use to roll up their own, you know?'

Their shared look of understanding confirmed the suspicion in both their minds.

'Definitely dope then,' she murmured, frowning, and laid a hand on his shoulder in reassurance. 'You did the right thing coming over. Well done. Young people need to stay sharp these days.'

'We had classes at school about drugs and stuff.'

'I'm pleased to hear it. You've just saved others from being affected. They're probably planning to sell the stuff around town. But right now we need to get the police. Who's the local?'

'Sergeant Peter Mills. He's the one came to school.' Tyler hardly drew breath before adding anxiously, 'I need to get back home. Be with my brothers. Make sure Zoe's okay.' He handed Maggie a scrap of paper. 'I wrote down the number plate of Jake's vehicle in case he leaves and the guy's address I was supposed to deliver to.'

'What did you tell Jake when you left?'

'That I needed time to think about it. Jake's a zombie. Zoe's mad to have anything to do with him. She was nicer before she met him.'

Maggie shrugged. Having met the girl now and being on the receiving end of sultry watchful eyes and long dark hair swishing about her shoulders, she knew the girl was self-possessed

168

and aware of her own power. Yet her swaggering attitude was also accompanied by an air of boredom and indifference.

'She's an attractive young woman.' Who desperately needed guidance. Maggie sighed. 'I'll phone Sergeant Mills now. You go home and try to stall Jake leaving. Keep him talking and get your brothers outside that house.'

'I'll try.'

'Tell the boys to go play while you talk to Jake.'

'What if he leaves?'

'Doesn't sound likely if Zoe's the magnet.' She tapped the slip of paper Tyler had given her. 'This registration number will find him and he'll most likely still have the drugs on him when you don't agree to deliver them. I'll make this call and be right over.'

Maggie grabbed for her phone as Tyler sped away on his bike. Sergeant Mills sounded young but capable when she explained the situation.

'Jake's known to us Ms Ellis. I'll be right there.'

A short time later, a police car quietly cruised into Stony Creek Way cul-de-sac and pulled into the Logan driveway behind Jake's battered old early model sedan, effectively stopping any hasty exit.

Maggie had been out the front of her cottage at the end of the driveway, waiting and pacing, but she stayed back as Sergeant Mills arrived, relieved to see the Logan boys all playing cricket in the paddock behind the house. Tyler had successfully convinced them both to play outdoors.

When the policeman went inside, Maggie called out and beckoned for Chris and Noah to

169

come to the cottage. With them safely in her care, they watched and waited from a distance. Some time later, Jake appeared first, handcuffed and complaining. Zoe trailed behind looking fearful and upset. Maggie felt deeply for her, no doubt coerced or at the very least influenced by Jake's attention and persuasion.

Before Sergeant Mills drove away he stopped his vehicle at the cottage and emerged. Maggie met him in her driveway, Tyler close behind.

'I spoke to you on the phone Ms Ellis. Are you the responsible adult for these boys?' he addressed Maggie.

She nodded. 'Until their father returns.'

'Pleased to meet you in person Ma'am. New in town?' She nodded. Mills smiled. 'Welcome to Tingara.'

'Thank you.'

'Need to take statements from you both. If you could bring Tyler down to the station I'd be obliged.'

'Sure.'

'It was only a small amount of drugs,' Pete explained. 'If it was a first offence, Jake would get a caution but since it's happened before, he'll be fined and recommended for counselling.'

'Zoe be okay?' Tyler asked.

Mills nodded. 'She'll get off with a warning but I'll go speak to her folks.' He squinted. 'It's a crime to allow people to bring drugs into your house but since Tyler raised the alarm, I'm sure we can prove no knowledge.' The sergeant extended his hand to Tyler. 'Appreciate your help, son.'

Tyler shook it, withholding a bashful grin of pride.

Maggie wrapped an arm around the boy's shoulders. 'I admire him so much for having the courage to come to me. Your father will be so proud,' she said sincerely.

After attending the station later to give witness statements, Maggie brought the boys home and they had fun putting their pizzas together in the homestead kitchen, ready for their father's return. He arrived home after dark but before the boys were in bed.

As always they heard the truck first descending gears down the Way and rumbling around the back of the house to pull up before Nick's massive vehicle shed.

When he stepped into the kitchen, his weary face naturally registered surprise at the sight of Maggie with his sons instead of Zoe.

'Maggie,' he nodded to her then said wryly, 'Nice surprise but it does raise a question.'

The appealing growth of stubble on his chin turned over her heart as much as the sight of him in tight dusty jeans, that familiar cowboy belt and soft blue shirt creased from a day's work to the contours of his powerful body.

Maggie sighed deeply before intending to respond but the boys were way ahead of her in a babble, all talking at once.

'Zoe's going to prison.'

'Jake had *drugs*.'

'The police car came.'

'Whoa.' Nick held up his hands, frowning. 'Maggie?'

171

So once Nick had cleaned up, Maggie produced his share of the remaining pizza slices and they all settled around the kitchen table to listen as she slowly recounted the afternoon's events.

Nick took it all in, gently cursed and then sent the older boys off to bed, spending time with Noah alone reassuring and explaining before returning to the kitchen where Maggie lingered.

Nick silently gestured to the outdoors and they sank into deck chairs out on the veranda to talk.

'Tyler's maturing and changing. He's grown a whole bunch more responsibility. I'm proud of him.'

'Have you told him that?'

Nick grinned and reached over to squeeze her hand. 'Of course.' He paused. 'To be honest, you've been such a positive influence on him. He respects you. I can't thank you enough for that and being up front and honest with my teenager.'

Maggie knew the compliment was genuine and probably a little difficult for him when initially he had been defensive on the subject of his singular role as the main parent for his sons. On reflection, she had wondered if she hadn't crossed a line that night of the cook up when she went out seeking to talk to Tyler. She hadn't meant to interfere but something deep in her heart had been touched and a spark of compassion ignited into action.

'Just trying to help and watch out for them all. They're great kids and a credit to you.'

'I'm tryin'. Takin' one day at a time.'

'All any of us can do.'

'Having you in our lives is making me realise how important it is that my boys have a female role model. They'll always have their mother but only distant I'm afraid. On a daily basis is another issue.'

'Seems to me you're doing just fine,' Maggie said quietly, rubbing her arms against the late spring chill.

Nick shuffled in his chair. 'I should let you go. Thanks again. For everything,' he said with meaning, springing to his feet.

'You're welcome.' She rose beside him, facing him, so close their bodies touched.

'I owe you,' he murmured, sliding an arm about her.

'Not necessary.'

He kissed her with such aching softness it buckled her knees. 'We'll see.'

'Another cook up would be fun,' she sighed in a daze, thinking nothing could be better than this flooding heat that filled her whenever he was around. Or the electricity they generated with a single touch. Or the awareness always of a craving for so much more.

'Oh I have something far more creative in mind than that,' he growled as they reluctantly drew apart.

'Oh? Well, night then,' was all Maggie could say as she stumbled away still reeling from that arousing kiss and what his hands did when they swept her body.

Her mind could only imagine what sex would

be like with this man but she was in no doubt that it would never be a disappointment. Oh, the promise of loving nights to come.

★ ★ ★

The next day Maggie decided it might prove worthwhile to have Nick and the boys over for dinner to see how they all worked together. Being a neighbour and friend was a whole world of difference to having a woman in the house who, in the boys' cases, was not their mother. Would they accept her in that role? All being well, if their love continued to progress, Nick had already hinted at becoming partners. Their strong mutual feelings were certainly heading in that direction.

Chris was easy going and agreeable. Noah still small and innocent enough to be unquestioning. And Tyler, holding resentment at first, had now come to trust her as proven by the drugs episode yesterday. His attitude and approval was of the greatest importance to Maggie for he was a sensitive soul beneath that outward shell.

In the following day or so, Maggie figured out how she could squeeze five people around a small table for four. By getting cosy, she guessed. And she was short one chair.

Then the menu needed consideration. All the Logans had healthy unfussy appetites so that shouldn't be a problem. The thought occurred that, in time, she could be feeding six on a daily basis. Good thing she was adept in a kitchen and loved cooking. Plus, remembering their cook up, she knew many hands would share the load.

So by mid-week, she gathered courage and wandered across the Way to face Nick again and invite the Logan men for dinner. A simple meal, she decided. The kind they might have if they were all sitting around the table like a family someday.

She strode up the driveway, *Lady* leaping around her, took the steps up to the veranda with confidence and knocked on the screen door. To heck with it, she thought, and walked right into the kitchen. She had timed her call for after school so she found Nick and Noah playing checkers at the table with the older boys playing Minecraft together on the television.

Nick flashed her a smile of such warmth and adoration, she grew flustered. 'Maggie, how are you doing?' And immediately pushed back his chair, rose and came to greet her.

She cleared her throat. 'Just fine. Hey boys.' They all acknowledged her or glanced in her direction in some way.

'What's up?' Nick teased.

She would love to kiss that smug smile off his face. 'Like to invite you all over to my cottage for dinner Saturday night. Nothing special. Pot luck. I owe you all a meal since the cook up.'

Nick was watching her so intently with a silly grin on his face, Maggie grew hot and self-conscious. Simply by her presence, she was telling him she had moved on and was ready for the start of more between them.

'I'm going over to Sam's place, remember?' Tyler complained from across the room.

Chris nudged him. 'Don't be rude. She might not ask us again. None of us will have to cook,' he emphasised.

'At least not for one night,' Maggie said, trying to be positive. It wouldn't work if they weren't all present.

'You can go to Sam's on Sunday, Tyler. Okay?' Nick scowled, his tone firm, demanding no objections. 'Right neighbourly of you Ms Ellis. We accept. All of us.' He glanced over to Tyler as he spoke.

Noah was sitting with his elbows on the table, his face in his hands staring at her the whole time since her arrival. She could see his short legs swinging beneath the table. 'What's for dessert?'

Maggie laughed. 'Not Bombe Alaska again. It's almost summer. Maybe lots of fresh healthy fruit.' His face crumpled with disappointment, so she added, 'With ice cream?'

His cute little face beamed. So easily pleased. If only life stayed so simple.

'I'll walk you out,' Nick offered. 'Noah, be back to finish our game shortly. No moving my counters while I'm gone,' he teased.

Out on the veranda, Nick wasted no time in taking a kiss. It wasn't as though Maggie would refuse. She'd only done it once but never again. Nick Logan could take every inch of her. If he didn't soon, she would embarrass herself and offer. Throw her middle aged self at him. It was getting so every parting was like cruel deprivation.

Once their romance passed the point of no

return with that final step, it would be impossible to hide her feelings. Maggie couldn't imagine not touching and kissing Nick in public or only showing their love and affection in private.

Was Nick holding back because of his sons? He had certainly given off nothing but positive signals.

'I missed you,' he whispered.

'It's only been three days.'

'Long enough. I was about to come over and take advantage of you.'

'Sounds exciting.'

Nick's playful mood was infectious and thrilling. With her demons being slayed, she felt more like the Maggie of her twenties. Lord, was it so long since she had allowed herself to have fun and feel happy? All due to this man. She smiled up into his melting brown eyes.

'You keep looking at me like that,' he growled, 'you're in big trouble.'

'Promises, promises,' she teased, moving away. 'Best get back. See you Saturday. Oh, by the way, can you bring an extra chair?'

He gave her a thumbs up, his brilliant grin totally electric.

★　★　★

Two evenings later, a deputation of males appeared at her back door in a murmur of deep voices. She heard Noah's excited chatter. They knocked, loudly, and busy draining steamed greens, shouted, 'Come on in.'

Suddenly her cottage was filled with company,

one extra chair, jostling boys, a grunted greeting from Tyler and Chris, a hug wrapped around her knees from Noah and, biggest surprise of all, a full on kiss from Nick in front of everyone that went way beyond a friendly peck.

The younger boys missed it but Tyler caught the intimacy and rolled his eyes.

She had taken care, washed and brushed her hair until it shone, and unashamedly dressed to bait. The mating game was on. Just so Nick was in no doubt of her feelings that she was available. But only for him.

He got the message. His eyes travelled all over her from the glossy hair to her fitted clinging jersey tunic top and all the way on down over shapely legs in jeggings to the strappy heels on her feet.

The boys were all smart in jeans and crisp shirts but their father took the prize. In tight black jeans that nestled snugly over his long muscled legs, matched with his favourite cowboy belt and buckle, and a silky cream shirt one shade darker than his sandy hair. With the tan on his skin of an outdoors man, he not only looked handsome but the hint of a masculine aftershave lingered about him as well.

He jolted her heart with a sudden glow of desire to find him at her side, wanting her as she did him, and giving her a virtual hug with a cheeky winning smile. Maggie felt cherished and special. Thank God she had moved to Tingara. Think of what she would have missed. Fate. Pure and simple.

Hours later, Maggie rated the evening one of

the best of her life. Noah insisted on sitting beside her and plonked himself down without question. Maggie's heart dissolved at the action. Nick swiftly claimed her other side and set about brushing his boots up against her feet under the table, and made sure their arms and knees touched at every opportunity.

The roast lamb went down a treat and Noah's eyes popped when instead of the promised fruit, she produced a sticky chocolate sauce pudding. With ice cream.

'You tricked me,' he giggled.

'No I didn't. If you remember, I said *maybe* we would have fruit.'

'Need to keep our wits about us boys. Maggie is one sharp lady.'

Maggie admitted to not being able to face the dishes so they were soaked and left in the sink. They all took it in turns playing board games, cards and Snap or Uno for Noah who happily snuggled with Milly on the sofa, the odd one out at times but content enough watching television.

When it grew late and Noah began yawning and looking sleepy, Nick said, 'Best take you boys home to bed.'

When they all rose without protest, Maggie masked her disappointment, having hoped for more but family came first.

Until Nick nodded toward the kitchen. 'Then I should come back and help Maggie with all these dishes.'

'Yeah, right,' she heard Tyler quip as they all shuffled out. 'Take care, Maggie,' the boy warned, his cheeky glance leaving her in no doubt exactly what he meant.

'Always do.' She grew embarrassed that these boys seemed to either know or sense something was up between herself and their father. She wondered how and her curiosity rose.

'Night, Maggie,' Chris grinned. Like his father, he didn't say much but he also rarely missed a thing.

As the older boys went on ahead, Nick lifted a drowsy Noah into his arms. The boy wrapped his arms about Nick's neck and murmured sleepily, 'Night, Maggie.'

'Night, champ.'

Nick whipped her a quick backward glance, his expression dark and dangerous. Maggie thrilled at the thought of what was to come.

She stayed a while in the mild evening, smelt the perfumes drifting to her from the fledgling garden and looked up into the star filled clear night sky. Lots to be grateful for and look forward to tonight. She rubbed her arms and returned indoors. Things to do before Nick returned.

Half an hour later when she heard his heavy tread on the outside path and the back door open, she was waiting for him.

His shadowed face registered surprise and mischief. 'You've done the dishes. Now I have no excuse to stay.'

'Not a problem. I'll give you one.' Standing in the sitting room, Maggie slowly unbuttoned her shirt, letting it slip over her shoulders before heading down the short hallway to her room.

Nick raised his eyebrows in expectation, her

message clear. 'Am I about to get lucky?'

'You'll never know if you don't come here to find out.'

'Maggie Ellis, you're Christmas early,' he drawled as he snapped out the lights and followed.

Like her, Maggie sensed Nick also wanted to take his time. It had been a while for both and they needed to savour this new discovery but their longing could barely be contained.

Pale moonlight streamed in her bedroom window, its soft light washing over Nick's beautiful muscled physique. This was the point of no return and Maggie would not have it any other way. It really didn't matter what happened after this, she would always have this staggering memory of this wonderful night.

As each explored and undressed the other with a passionately slow reverence, a wanton drive built in her and it was clear Nick was ready for action, too. With his caresses and gaze all over her body, Maggie's fire was impossible to dowse.

When their naked bodies were finally free of clothes and revealed to each other, he hauled her against him. Pressed together, Maggie was stunned by Nick's gorgeous body and his dark eyes told her he worshipped her every shapely curve and inch of glowing skin.

He lowered her back onto the bed, kissing her mouth, licking and teasing her already stimulated breasts, her nipples hard with excitement, then moving lower to hidden places.

When he moved over her, Maggie sighed. They fit perfectly together. Was this right or what? She had never known such tender considerate loving and gave herself completely in return. Joined together they rode the building wave of need both finding release and breathing with heavy satisfaction.

Nick slid away, cuddling Maggie against him, drawing the doona over their cooling skin.

'I love you, Maggie,' he whispered.

Tears pricked her eyes. 'Me, too.'

She tilted her face up to kiss him, hardly able to believe that he loved and wanted her with equal heart. Far from feeling self-conscious of her comely figure, naturally slimmer these days as a result of more physical activity outdoors, Maggie revelled in Nick's admiration.

He groaned, started nibbling her again and proceeded to show her exactly how he felt all over again. Nick stirred her soul. Around him, Maggie was stimulated but also at peace with herself and the world.

Amazing that this sexy man had stolen so quietly into her life, supported her in every way in the transition from city to country and with whom she felt so alive, she knew she never wanted to leave him.

In the early hours before daylight, Maggie woke from the deepest most sensuous sleep to see Nick's face beside her on the pillow just staring.

'Can't you sleep?' she murmured. He shook his head. 'Need to get home to the boys?' Her hopes deflated.

'Soon, but before I do I have something for you.'

'Not that,' Nick chuckled when she searched under the doona.

'You're not letting me go back to sleep, are you? Can't it wait?'

'Nope.'

'Does this need brandy or tea?'

'Neither,' he drawled, rolled his warm body over and reached down to his jeans on the floor, retrieving scraps of paper from a pocket.

He sat up against the bedhead. 'Come here,' he patted the space beside him and snapped on the lamp.

Their bare bodies snuggled together beneath the half pulled up cover, still necessary on these cool nights before the onset of another Australian summer.

'Ooh, I love surprises.'

# 12

With Nick's voice vibrating against her ear as she laid her head against his chest, he said, 'Being together is a decision for you and me but I've talked to the boys, got three nods of approval and asked them to write something for you.'

Maggie playfully punched his chest. 'So that's why they all looked like they knew something tonight.' She frowned. 'Nods of approval for . . . what exactly?'

'Patience.'

'You've asked them before you asked me?' she pretended to be wounded but was secretly excited and holding her breath over daring to hope what was coming.

'All in good time. Logans do things as a family. Read the notes.' He handed her three folded pieces of paper.

Maggie opened the first.

*Please say yes. For my Dad,* was all Christopher wrote, signing his name. A boy of few words. She swallowed back tears at the simple plea.

Tyler's appeal was vague yet clear to her in the light of his emotional journey and penned in a casual scrawly hand. *It will be cool having a new mum in our home. You make everyone feel like you care.* A veiled reference to his mother. Maggie's heart cracked a little that Rachel would probably never play a big part in his life. She determined to give him all the love and support he ever needed.

The final one was in the same handwriting as Tyler's. You smell nice when you read me stories in bed. You love cooking so we won't have to do as much. I like being with you and going to your greenhouse when I need you. I know you're not my real mother but I love you already so can you please pretend. P.S. Tyler wrote down my words for me.

It was no revelation to Maggie that she already adored this child and his big brothers, and had fallen deeply in love with their father. She had always thought she wanted a family and children of her own. How utterly uninformed she was in the ways of the world. Since dealing with her issues she hadn't realised even existed, thanks to Nick's wise observations, for the first time in her life nothing else mattered. She wanted all of them in her life. Father *and* sons. Ready-made.

And if children were, or were not, a blessing in their future, then that would be okay, too.

Plunged deep in sweet thoughts after being engrossed in the boys' beautiful notes, Maggie focused on Nick beside her again. While she was distracted, he had somehow plucked a small box from thin air or his trouser pocket again. She grinned and wanted to grab it from his hands but curbed her excitement.

'Knowing you now and on my instructions, I had Emma create this for you.' As he gently pressed it into her hands, he murmured, 'Maggie Ellis, from the deepest part of my heart, this gift means love. Everyone wants it. I guess it's the

185

closest thing we humans have on earth to magic. I can't live without you. I need you and love you. My boys love you,' he quipped. 'Will you marry me?'

'In a heartbeat. To the moon and back.' She grabbed him for a kiss. 'Luckily I only need to move next door.'

Because her hands were shaking, Nick slowly pushed open the box lid. Maggie gasped. A faceted amethyst heart edged either side with butterflies, their wings inlaid with diamonds, nestled among black velvet. The gardening theme was not lost on her.

'You're a sensitive person,' Nick said, 'so I chose amethyst which is apparently not only a stone of the spirit for calm, balance and peace but it's also the stone of St. Valentine and faithful love.'

Maggie pressed her hands to her face at the sight of this utterly gorgeous dream ring. 'Oh my God,' she breathed.

She trembled all over as Nick slid it onto her finger and she smiled through the happiest of tears. They kissed long and slow to seal the deal.

And then, just to heap more happiness into her life, he murmured, 'I've been thinking about it and I'm feeling I would want more children with you. *Our* children.'

Maggie gasped. 'Nick?'

'Hell Maggie, you're a smart woman,' he chuckled, nuzzling her hair. 'Can't make it much plainer. You're a beautiful woman inside and out. You're the woman I'm truly meant to be with. So, I not only want to marry you and have lots of sex but babies, too. *Ours*,' he emphasised, and she knew exactly what he meant. 'Something wearing pink might be nice for a change, don't you think?' he teased.

Maggie stared at him, dumbfounded. She was so overcome with love for this man. Tears pooled in her eyes and rolled down her face. 'Hell, Nick, you sure know how to turn on a woman. I'm nearly forty. We better keep going then, huh? Hope the timer hasn't run out on my ovaries.'

'Maggie Ellis,' he growled, dragging her closer, 'you're so damned sexy and luscious, I doubt that's gonna be a problem.'

After an exciting long kiss fuelled with heat and desire, Nick groaned, admitting he wanted to linger quite a while longer to take advantage of his fiancée again before moaning with regret, 'Must get back to my sons.'

'Of course.' But she clung to him, deliberately delaying the parting before he dressed and jogged home next door.

★  ★  ★

Next morning, happily weary from a lost night's sleep, to Nick's surprise Tyler bailed him up in the kitchen before his two younger sons appeared. 'What took so long last night?'

As if his teen son didn't know. 'Maggie needed a little . . . persuasion.'

Tyler shook his head and said wryly, 'Dad, she was a sure thing.'

The knowing look they exchanged and mutual male bond of the moment brought father and son closer together than they had been for some time. A breakthrough when Nick reconnected with Tyler man-to-man. And for the first time in a while he hugged his son again who, for once, didn't stiffen or resist.

The responses to the Ellis-Logan engagement were varied and expected. Maggie told her parents first. Mike and Carol Ellis were overjoyed. Her mother asked if she was truly in love, a note of caution in her voice. Maggie knew exactly what she meant for Carol had travelled the long road of her unhappy previous partnership along with her daughter.

Maggie was able to fully reassure her.

'Then that's all we need to know, dear.'

Her parents got it. For, after forty years together, they already knew about the strength and dedication needed in loving for a lifetime.

'It's worth waiting for the right one,' Carol had said on more than one occasion before.

'Isn't it just?' Maggie said now in reply, finally understanding.

Her brother Paul and sister-in-law, Debbie, on the other hand rudely displayed their shock.

'A truck driver!' Debbie said.

'Are you sure, Mags?' Paul queried, his tone heaped with doubt. 'You're not on the rebound? You barely know this guy.'

Ah, but that was where he was wrong. 'Yes, isn't it amazing,' Maggie said with genuine excitement. 'I knew the moment we met.'

She refused to let anyone dampen her happiness and contentment gained through the power of a man's true love.

Penny's reaction made Maggie feel only pity and disappointment. 'Are you sure you're not making another mistake?'

Maggie winced and tuned out after that, sad that her one time best friend couldn't be more positive and happy. But in an evil moment of mischief she hoped Penny's gossip found its way to her ex and his pregnant babe.

By comparison, Emma Webster and Hannah Bennett, the two girlfriends she had come to know as wives of Nick's best mates, both screamed with excitement when told the news.

As Maggie looked on, beaming, they high fived each other. 'We knew it!' they said smugly.

'It was so hard keeping Nick's secret,' Emma admitted. 'That man came to me with such love in his eyes and heart. He adores you, Maggie. And you're a perfect match for each other.'

'Yes, I agree,' Hannah said. 'I haven't known Nick as long but I can see you bagged a good one there, Maggie.'

The three women lolled about on her couches in the blacksmith cottage she and Mal called home.

'We all did,' Emma laughed.

After hugs all around, fizz appeared and champagne flutes filled. There always seemed to be a cold bottle chilling in the fridge and an excuse to pop one open.

'For me,' Emma said, 'it all started when I returned to Tingara after living and working in Sydney for years and my marriage broke down. I came back to town to lick my wounds and hide.' She glanced across at Hannah. 'Can you believe,

Gran tried to pair me with Will but we'd been mates at primary school and that's the only way I've ever thought of him.

'Then Mal came into town last autumn restoring *Clovelly* on Wattle Gully Road, his grandparents' old home, and we sparked. Next thing you know, Hannah does a random stab on a map and crosses the world in a house swap to St. Anne's last winter, just a few doors down Gum Tree Lane from Will. We all saw the attraction there straight away. Will followed Hannah back to England, marries her and while they're off travelling, Maggie buys *Lakeside* and moves in next door to Nick! Within months, boom, they're an item. Who knew?'

The women clinked champers flutes in a toast and chattered on.

★ ★ ★

When it came to planning the wedding and Nick pointed out his family was large and scattered all over the country, Maggie simply said, 'Let's invite them all and see who shows up. Those that really want to be here will make it.'

Maggie also sneakily invited Penny with a *plus one* knowing it was unlikely.

'Any thoughts on the ceremony?' Nick asked.

'In my garden. With a big reception marquee at your place.'

He nodded. 'What about your cottage?'

'I'll keep the nursery business. The cottage could become a cosy couples B&B or a place to park friends and relatives when they come to visit.'

So one hot Australian summer afternoon two months later, Tingara was treated to yet another wedding. While the town bloomed with colour, friends and family gathered to witness the exchange of vows between Margaret Carol Ellis and Nicholas Charles Logan beneath an arbour in *Lakeside* cottage gardens with the gurgling music of Stony Creek in the background.

A beaming Maggie strolled through her flowery paradise crammed with summer colour on her father's arm toward her hero, Nick, the man of her heart and dreams.

Three smartly dressed boys stood beside their father, grinning, alongside his best mates, Mal and Will. Emma and Hannah, having preceded the bride, stood opposite their menfolk in long watercolour floral dresses and carrying luxuriant summer posies.

It seemed to Maggie that the groom only had eyes and smiles for his love. Her. She glowed at the sight of the tall man only steps away now, his sandy hair gleaming in the dappled sun, cheeky and gorgeous in a tailored dark suit, the crisp white shirt highlighting his sun browned face and stunning larrikin smile.

His possessive gaze prowled hungrily over her ivory sequined gown with its heart neckline and revealing cut out back which, as yet, he could not see. The waistline was nipped in just enough to showcase her enviable figure with a clutch of lace flowing freely out from her waist to catch tendrils of lavender at the path's edge as she passed. A long trailing creation of frothy white *Susan* roses and greenery from the bush in her garden quivered in her hands.

'I love you so much,' Nick whispered passionately when, gracious and feminine, she finally reached him.

And then, after the formalities and intimate vows, he was hers and dissolving her in his arms for a kiss. The guests stood and applauded.

Maggie's parents were the first to hug and congratulate them, followed by virtually everyone else.

Paul and Debbie turned up their noses at the rustic country wedding. Later when their oldest daughter, Melissa, made eyes at handsome teen, Tyler, who bashfully returned her interest, controlling mother Debbie was heard to say, 'He's not for you, dear,' and drew the girl away.

Maggie smiled to herself and thought it best not to mention that she had deliberately seated Melissa and Tyler next to each other at the reception!

Mike and Carol admired Nick on sight. As Maggie expected. And were over the moon to have instantly acquired three new grandchildren. Maggie pointedly assured them they could visit any time and stay in the cottage next door.

Nick counted all of his siblings in attendance, bringing a tribe of nieces and nephews with them. He proudly introduced them all to his wife. Maggie literally embraced them all, which took a while, and apologised if she forgot any names.

Ivy Ashford's wedding gift was to hand over a large thick envelope enclosing her nursery shop keys and the title to the property. Maggie gasped and burst into tears. To which Ivy merely muttered, 'Better make a go of it.'

'Where will you live?' Maggie sniffed as Nick handed her a big blue handkerchief.

'Upstairs above the shop in my flat. Be keeping an eye on you.'

Nick's mother, Liz, her weary face lined but smiling, made apologies for his father, claiming him *unwell*.

'Drunk most likely,' Nick murmured.

'Charlie is staying on the farm but I've moved into a flat in town. Time I retired.' Liz Logan announced with a wink.

Maggie noticed Nick quietly smiling at that welcome news.

'She's finally left him,' he said later.

After a discussion, it was decided that if she wished his mother stay on in Tingara for a well-deserved overdue holiday in the new *Lakeside B&B*. For as long as she pleased.

The only other absentee on the day was Maggie's friend, Penny, who had sent an inability to attend.

Maggie was gutted and wondered why their former friendship now meant nothing. And she might never know. It only briefly occurred to her to reach out to Penny, contact her to talk or send a letter. But friendship went both ways and Maggie knew she was done with being the one to make the effort for, in hindsight now, she realised, that was how it had been. Always scrambling to sustain it.

Some people entered your life briefly, some stayed longer, and yet others were destined to be a part of it forever. No matter what.

Like those around her now, Maggie thought, looking about the crowd of similarly happy laughing guests celebrating this awesome wedding day. For she would remember it as nothing less.

She gazed up dreamily at Nick and smiled as he held her in his arms, dancing. He hadn't come crashing into her life but snuck up quietly like a gently falling night. For that was his way.

He calmed her and brought her love and peace. She knew in her heart when they were both old and grey, she would still be with him and truly loved.

'I love you, Nick Logan,' she murmured.

'Do tell.' He grinned and they stopped dancing to kiss. 'I kind of guessed.'

'Just so you know.'

# Epilogue

One year later

'This is just crazy,' Emma Webster beamed, sitting up in her hospital bed in Tingara Medical Centre looking youthful and fit the day after giving birth to a son, Oliver, and future little playmate and half-brother for seven year old, Daniel.

Husband Mal sat on the bed beside her.

'You have two builder's apprentices lined up there already, mate,' Nick teased him, flashing a devilish grin between the man's two sons.

'Yes, there's been quite an explosion of babies in the community,' Maggie Logan laughed.

'How many are you planning?' Emma nodded toward Nick, protectively cuddling one pink-wrapped twin bundle in each arm named Grace and Charlotte who had arrived impatient and early one month ago. They had only just been released and allowed home from hospital a few days before.

Zoe, who had long since ditched her boyfriend Jake and finished school, was on hand to help as much as possible. And big brother Tyler was proving to be capable, moving between nursery and kitchen as needed.

The Logans were doing fine.

The darling little female newbies slept through all the noise and chatter in the hospital room. Occasionally, the girls squirmed or yawned but with three energetic older brothers, they were adjusting early.

'As many as my ovaries will allow until they shrivel,' Maggie lowered her voice with a side glance to her husband.

'I heard that,' he drawled.

'That's not fair,' Emma protested. 'You're already ahead of the game with three boys. That's five to one in your favour.'

'Yeah, kinda got lucky there, huh? The new homestead wing extension is done now, thanks to Mal.' She glanced across to him on the other side of the bed.

'And with a labour of only a few hours even with twins, how clever is that?' Emma said.

'They did rather arrive in a rush,' Maggie smiled serenely.

'Next time we'll leave earlier,' Nick said with good humour.

'If they are all so easy, why wouldn't you?' Emma said. 'Oliver here took all night.' She looked down adoringly at her sleeping son in his hospital crib beside her. 'But he was so worth it. I haven't asked. Is there a history of twins in either of your families?' she glanced up at Maggie.

She nodded. 'Apparently in mine.'

She cast a nostalgic look across to Nick and caught his gaze but didn't elaborate. Today was not the right moment. Time enough for explanations of her lost twin all those years ago to their friends in the future.

'Well we couldn't have planned this better if we tried, could we?' Hannah Bennett said in her lovely English accent as she waddled into the room, tummy bulging, her arms filled with flowers and gifts for the latest new mother among their friends.

Emma looked around behind her. 'Where's Will?'

'Painting the cradle he made. Literally. With princesses and animals in rainbow colours to cover either eventuality. Won't have a bar of pink or blue. Says he doesn't want his child to be stereotyped.' Hannah glowed with contentment.

'Typical Will, not wanting to know if it's going to be boy or girl.'

'I don't mind,' Hannah smiled. 'It will be a brilliant surprise.'

'You're going to need my hospital bed any day now,' Emma said.

'I hope so. I'm kind of done with this whole nine month waiting thing,' she groaned, rubbing her back.

'Just think,' Maggie said, 'in five years' time all our children will be trotting off to school together. And our social dinners promise to include lots more children.'

Amid the laughter that followed, Mary Hamilton arrived to meet her newest great grandchild, bearing an armful of blue-wrapped gifts. Ivy Ashford shuffled in behind.

While kisses and coos over baby Oliver were exchanged in the Webster and Hamilton families, Maggie hugged Ivy. 'You left the shop?' she teased.

Ivy sent her a dark glance in the direction of Nick and their twin daughters. 'I was hoping to retire,' she muttered.

Maggie knew Ivy had no such intention and despite the florist's protests, she and Mary had arranged help in the shop for her. 'Not just yet, Ivy,' Maggie quipped. 'You're far too young.'

To which the elderly woman had the grace to shake her head and try a smile.

With an arm comfortably around Ivy's shoulders and over the buzz of conversation in the room, Maggie's gaze drifted out beyond the hospital window in reflection and one morning six months earlier.

★ ★ ★

Emma, Hannah and Maggie had gathered for their usual regular catch up for coffee and cake but, on that day, were not in the bakery café as sometimes happened but sitting around Emma's kitchen table in the blacksmith's cottage.

Both being tea addicts, Hannah poured a big mug for herself and Maggie.

Emma turned up her nose at her usual coffee. 'Just make mine black today, thanks.'

'You okay?' Maggie asked. 'Tummy bug or something?'

Emma look abashed and said, 'I have something in my stomach but it isn't a bug!'

'You don't mean-?'

She nodded, releasing her excitement. 'Did the stick test thing and been to the doc for confirmation.'

Squeals of laughter erupted from Hannah and Maggie who looked at each other and spoke together.

'Actually — '

'You know what — ?'

'You first,' Maggie said generously to Hannah who she could see was bursting with news, too. No, she thought. Surely it couldn't be? Three pairs of wide eyes and gaping mouths turned in every direction.

'You too?'

'You're not!'

'This is crazy.'

'We're all preggers?'

'Damn, we can't crack the champers.'

'We will in six months when they all arrive.'

They all laughed. A dreamily smiling Maggie turned her attention back to the hospital room, her adoring husband and two beautiful daughters, and the potential for not only the Logans to become an even bigger family.

What amazing journeys they had all experienced, she marvelled. Like the autumn leaves of Tingara that had helped Emma and Mal find each other, and the winter holiday in the small town that brought English woman Hannah virtually to Will's door, spring's promise and glory in country Australia had blossomed into love for Maggie and Nick, too.

Now, in the following summer, they were all blessed with binding loves, growing families and unknown futures ahead. In Tingara. Together.

Grace — or was it Charlotte? — started to grizzle. Maggie still grew confused, not yet knowing her identical daughters apart and her maternal instinct tugged into action.

'Time for another feed,' she laughed. 'That's

all I seem to do these days.'

Everyone hugged and said temporary good-byes, wishing Hannah well for her imminent happy event.

In a timely arrival, student nurse Zoe bustled into view through the doorway, trim in her uniform. A midwifery career was her ultimate goal but, for now, she was training to become an enrolled nurse and reached out to lovingly scoop Grace into her arms.

'I'm off duty now. Heading home, are we?'

Zoe and Nick carrying a baby each and Maggie strolling contentedly behind walked out to the new larger Logan family vehicle, the summer sunshine drenching them all with warmth. Reminding Maggie of that special day a year ago when she had married the man of her heart and soul.

She and Nick shared an indulgent reminiscent smile, buckled their daughters into their capsules and climbed into the car to embrace another busy day and the trials and blessings that had brought them to this moment.

Grateful for the journey so far, their profound love and every single day to come.

*Other titles published by Ulverscroft:*

## HANNAH'S HOLIDAY

### Noelene Jenkinson

Workaholic accountant Hannah Charles takes a leap of faith and a much needed holiday in a house swap from the Cotswolds to converted St. Anne's Church in Tingara, Australia. Easy-going architect-cum-artist Will Bennett has family estrangement issues and lives an alternative lifestyle in the small country town. Can an untidy artist and a guilt-ridden runaway overcome their differences and distance to let love grow?

# OUTBACK TREASURE

## Noelene Jenkinson

Wrongly disgraced and her career left in tatters, palaeontologist Darcy Manning embarks on a mission to expose the fossil smuggling syndicate responsible, to clear her name and reputation. But how will she resist alluring country boy and fellow fossil-hunter Mitch Beaumont, when he is such a crucial piece of the puzzle? Set at Matilda Station in outback Queensland, *Outback Treasure* is one woman's story of a search for truth and justice, even at the risk of her own heart.

# KITTY MCKENZIE

## AnneMarie Brear

1864: Suddenly left as the head of the family, Kitty McKenzie must find her inner strength to keep her family together against the odds. Evicted from their resplendent home in the fashionable part of York after her parents' deaths, Kitty must fight the legacy of bankruptcy and homelessness to secure a home for her and her siblings. Through sheer willpower and determination she grabs opportunities with both hands, from working on a clothes and rag stall in the market to creating a teashop for the wealthy. Her road to happiness is fraught with obstacles of hardship and despair, but she refuses to let her dream of a better life for her family die. She soon learns that love and loyalty bring their own rewards.